"My Father!

"Don't make me laugh. You would never let him or anybody else stand in the way of what you wanted. Which only leads me to one conclusion. You didn't want me." She jumped to her feet.

Bram stood also. "That isn't true. I wanted you very much. And if you can't accept that, your recollection of that evening isn't as clear as mine is."

Beth held up her hand. "Excuse me—you're right. You wanted me physically; I remember that very well. What you didn't want was a relationship with a clinging teenager who would foul up your plans to have a girl in every port."

"Is that what you think?"

Beth stared at him. "Isn't that right? I wanted it all, and you weren't ready to give it."

Dear Reader,

Welcome to Silhouette! Our goal is to give you hours of unbeatable reading pleasure, and we hope you'll enjoy each month's six new Silhouette Desires. These sensual, provocative love stories are both believable and compelling—sometimes they're poignant, sometimes humorous, but always enjoyable.

Indulge yourself. Experience all the passion and excitement of falling in love along with our heroine as she meets the irresistible man of her dreams and together they overcome all obstacles in the path to a happy ending.

If this is your first Desire, I hope it'll be the first of many. If you're already a Silhouette Desire reader, thanks for your support! Look for some of your favorite authors in the coming months: Stephanie James, Diana Palmer, Dixie Browning, Ann Major and Doreen Owens Malek, to name just a few.

Happy reading!

Isabel Swift
Senior Editor

SDRL-7/85

DOREEN OWENS MALEK
Reckless Moon

Silhouette Desire

Published by Silhouette Books New York

America's Publisher of Contemporary Romance

For all the reckless hearts among my readers.

SILHOUETTE BOOKS
300 E. 42nd St., New York, N.Y. 10017

Copyright © 1985 by Doreen Owens Malek

Distributed by Pocket Books

ISBN: 0-373-0 5222-7

First Silhouette Books printing July, 1985

10 9 8 7 6 5 4 3 2 1

America's Publisher of Contemporary Romance

Printed in the U.S.A.

DOREEN OWENS MALEK

is an attorney and former teacher who decided on her current career when she sold her fledging novel to the first editor who read it. She has been writing ever since. Born and raised in New Jersey, she has lived throughout the Northeast and now makes her home in Pennsylvania.

Books by Doreen Owens Malek

Silhouette Romance

The Crystal Unicorn #363

Silhouette Special Edition

A Ruling Passion #154

Silhouette Desire

Native Season #86
Reckless Moon #222

Silhouette Intimate Moments

The Eden Tree #88
Devil's Deception #105

1

He's here," Mindy said breathlessly, pulling the door shut behind her.

Beth Forsyth swallowed the lump in her throat and tried to appear calm. "Who's here?" she asked neutrally, reaching for her hairbrush.

"Bram Curtis, who else?" Mindy replied, exasperated. "I told you he'd show."

"I didn't think he'd have the nerve."

Mindy smiled impishly. "Yes, you did. The one thing Bram never lacked was nerve."

Beth tried to feign indifference as she smoothed her hair into place. "How does he look?" she asked casually.

Mindy sighed, adjusting the hem of her gown. "Wonderful," she said wistfully. "He has a beard now, and his hair is longer, but it just makes him look more . . . rakish . . . or something." Her eyes met Beth's in the mirror. "He's still the sexiest thing you ever saw."

Beth's expression indicated that she didn't consider this bulletin good news.

Mindy shook her head. "Look, Bethany, if you were hoping that he'd gotten fat or bald, forget it. He looks different, but the impact is the same." She paused, and added, "Only more so."

Beth fiddled with the pearl button on her lace cuff. More so. How was that possible? Bram had made such an impression originally that he had inhabited her dreams for ten years.

She felt Mindy's hands on her shoulders. "Relax," her friend said quietly. "It was a long time ago. You were a kid then; a lot of things are different now. You're all grown up, you're a lawyer with a career to build, and your father is dead. Both of you have been away; hardly anyone remembers the reason you left. So forget it. Tough it out and the evening will be over before you know it."

"Are there many people downstairs?" Beth asked Mindy.

Mindy nodded. "A full house. Everybody showed to give your sister the royal send-off."

Beth's sister, Marion, had gotten married in New York, and then returned home to Connecticut for the open house that would be her local wedding reception. She had issued a general invitation to the neighbors, but it had not occurred to Beth that Bram might be a guest until she heard he had returned to Suffield from his latest stint in the merchant marine. And the word was, with his stepmother gone and his father in bad health, this time he would stay.

"Do you think this dress is right for me?" Beth asked anxiously, adjusting the lace bib.

"You're beautiful," Mindy said warmly. "You look perfectly lovely. Now stop fussing and come with me. The dress is fine."

"It's so frilly," Beth said worriedly. "I fell in love with it when I saw it, but now I don't know." She turned to crane her neck at the full-length pier glass on the other side of the bedroom. "You don't think it makes me look like Lillie Langtry?"

Mindy rolled her eyes. "Lillie Langtry was a legendary beauty; if you look like her you're in good shape."

"She's been dead for fifty years," Beth said, frowning at her reflection.

Mindy stamped her foot. "You're stalling! I never should have told you he was here."

"I'd have killed you if you didn't."

"I'm going to kill *you* if you don't get a move on. Marion has been asking for you for half an hour. She's going to think something is wrong with you."

"Something *is* wrong with me. I have to face a man I haven't seen since I was sixteen, the person responsible for my being packed off to boarding school in suspicious haste by my outraged father, and I'm dressed like a character in an Edwardian farce."

"That's it," Mindy said, throwing up her hands. "I'm leaving. You can hide up here for the rest of the night, but I'm not going to cover for you. Good-bye." Mindy made for the door.

"All right," Beth called after her. "I'm coming."

9

Mindy halted.

"You're still a terrible bully," Beth grumbled.

"I've been practicing," Mindy replied. "While you were off getting an education, I was whipping two preschoolers into line."

Beth put her hand on Mindy's arm. "What am I going to say to him?" she asked softly.

Mindy opened the bedroom door and pushed Beth through it. "Bethany, when were you ever at a loss for words?" she said, walking into the hall.

Beth's eyes roamed the crowd of well-wishers as she and Mindy descended the spiral staircase of her father's house. It belonged to Beth and her sister now, with their mother and father both dead, but Marion would return to New York with her stockbroker husband and Beth would live in it alone. She had plans to convert a ground-floor wing into an office for her budding practice, but that was before she found out that Bram Curtis was back in Suffield. For good, Marion said. It would be difficult to stay here now, with Bram at his father's place just down the road. He hadn't been back since the night Beth's father found them together, and now he had turned up just as Beth was settling in to start her firm. Damn the man. It was just like him to reappear at the least opportune moment.

Bram was not among the group milling about the front hall, nor was he in the living room or dining room that led off from it to the right and left. Beth wandered into the kitchen at the back of the house with Mindy's daughter, Tracy, clinging to her skirts. Mindy, seizing the moment, had vanished.

Marion was standing at the sink, breaking ice cubes into a bucket. She turned at Beth's approach.

"There you are," she greeted her sister. "Help me with this; my arms are broken from trying to get these beastly things out of the trays."

Beth took over the task, saying, "I don't know why you didn't let us cater this thing. You're the only bride I've ever seen who's waiting on people at her own reception."

Marion got a Popsicle from the freezer and gave it to Tracy, who proceeded to smear the sticky concoction all over her organdy dress.

"I hate strangers wandering around Daddy's house," Marion replied. "It's nicer for us to give the party ourselves."

"Mindy is going to be very happy when she sees that child," Beth commented dryly. Tracy now had a chocolate mustache.

"It's keeping her occupied," Marion said darkly. She peered at Beth's face. "Bram Curtis is here," she announced.

"So everyone has told me," Beth replied, "but I haven't seen him."

"I have." Marion bit her lip. It made her look like their mother, who had used the same gesture when she was concerned.

"Don't worry, Marion," Beth said. "I'm not going to spoil your party. I will be very civil, I promise you." She handed her sister the ice, then refilled the trays at the sink.

"You're not the one I'm worried about," Marion said. "He always was wild, but you should see him now. He has a beard, and when he smiles, those teeth against that midnight hair . . ." she trailed off, unable to complete the thought. She took the trays, putting them away.

"Maybe we should lock up the silver," Beth whispered.

Marion stared at her. "How can you make jokes, after what he did to you?"

"He didn't do anything *to* me, Marion. In Daddy's immortal words, 'It takes two to tango.'"

"Daddy never was very original," Marion giggled.

Tracy dropped the remains of her Popsicle on her left shoe and began to wail.

"Oh, dear," Marion said. She took the dishrag from the sink and started to wipe ineffectually at the spreading brown stain.

Mindy appeared in the doorway, summoned by Tracy's cries, and scooped the little girl into her arms.

"I gave her the Popsicle," Marion said guiltily.

Mindy shifted Tracy to one arm and waved the other. "Never mind, if it wasn't this it would have been something else; she always winds up filthy at the end of one of these things. Where's your husband?"

"Making drinks on the patio. I'm supposed to be getting him ice."

"I'll go with you," Mindy said, and the two women went out together, leaving Beth alone. She threaded her way through the guests on the lower level, nodding and smiling, and finally sought refuge in her father's study, a small room behind the garage at the back of the house. Lined with books, the walls hung with family memorabilia, it was her favorite place to think.

When she opened the door a man turned from the fireplace, where he had been leaning on the stone mantel. There was a half-finished drink in his hand. Beth looked at him, and a decade dissolved in an instant.

"Bram," Beth said, striving to regain her shattered equilibrium. "What are you doing in here?"

He saluted her with his glass. "Isn't it obvious? I'm crashing your party."

Beth closed the door, shutting out the din of conversation from the rest of the house. "You're not crashing," she said evenly. "The neighbors were invited, and you're a neighbor. I want to know why you're in this room, that's all."

His black brows shot up into his hair. "I got lost?" he suggested.

Beth merely looked at him.

"Came to borrow a dictionary?" His dark eyes mocked her.

Beth waited.

He shrugged, draining his glass. "Well, I guess that rules out drawn here by forces beyond my control and driven to return to the scene of the crime." He slapped his empty glass on the mantel and surveyed her archly. "This room holds a rather significant memory for me. You, too?"

Beth's heart thumped against her breastbone. "I would rather forget what happened between us in here."

He rocked slightly on his heels. "Ah, yes, the sweet little teenager seduced by the big, bad sailor." He took a step toward her. "I suppose that's the way you prefer to think of it. Except that isn't quite true, is it, Bethany? You and I, we know what really happened."

"I don't want to go over all of that again," Beth said hoarsely. She still reacted to the sound of his voice saying her name.

"I'll bet you don't," he said softly, moving closer

13

yet. She tried not to meet his eyes, but her gaze was drawn to his, mesmerized.

He did look different from the way she remembered him, but his attractiveness was hardly diminished by the change. Ten years before he'd been clean-shaven, with close-cropped wavy hair. Now the lower part of his face was covered by a short black beard, and his raven hair had grown out into dark wings that covered his ears and curled over his collar. Trust Bram to adopt longer hair when it had really passed out of style; he always liked to be different. But the cola-brown eyes, the thick, dark lashes, the strong white teeth were all the same. And the slim, powerful body, clad in a dark suit in honor of the occasion, was as lean and agile as she recalled. Beth ached to go to him, but she backed away.

He laughed softly. "You had more guts the last time I saw you," he said. "You've changed."

"You were drunk the last time I saw you," Beth replied. "You haven't changed at all."

His eyes widened, and the fading evening sun coming through the window lightened them to the color of milk chocolate. "Drunk," he said, indignant. "Certainly not. I had a couple of nips for courage, nothing much."

"You needed courage to face me?" Beth asked, watching him.

He turned away, not answering. Then, after a moment, "Maybe I needed courage to face the memories in this room." He looked back at her. "I never wanted your father to send you away, Bethany."

Beth said nothing.

"I went to see him the next day and tried to talk him

out of it," Bram added. "As soon as I heard his plan, I tried to dissuade him."

Beth couldn't conceal her surprise.

Bram nodded. "I didn't think he told you about that. You assumed I'd just abandoned you to your hapless fate, didn't you?"

"Does it matter what I thought?" Beth asked wearily, pushing back a strand of her hair. "It was a long time ago. I was just a willful, impulsive child, and you were just . . ."

"A full-grown man who didn't know the meaning of the word 'restraint,'" Bram finished dryly. "When a sixteen-year-old girl gets together with a twenty-five-year-old merchant seaman, you don't have to tell me who's responsible."

"That's not what you said a few minutes ago," Beth replied, reeling. She now remembered how he could blithely switch tracks in a second, leaving her to stumble after him in a desperate struggle to understand.

"A few minutes ago I was smarting from the impact of your frosty reception," he stated flatly.

Beth didn't know how to respond to that, so she asked, "Are you home to stay? I heard you might be."

He made a dismissive gesture. "My father appears to need me to run the business, and since my dear stepmother has at last left him for good, there seems to be no reason why I shouldn't stay." His eyes drifted away from her face, looking into the distance. "I've finally tired of roaming the globe, Bethany." Then he grinned suddenly, his magnificent teeth flashing. "The prodigal son has returned."

"Your father must be happy about that."

Bram shrugged. "As long as Anabel remains in Palm Beach, I'll stick. He never missed me before, but now he's too sick to get along without me, so I've become necessary."

His acid tone regarding his family hadn't changed either. Bram's mother had died when he was small, and when Bram was fifteen his father, at that time fifty, had married Anabel, who was half his age. Bram's enmity for his stepmother was legendary, and their disagreements had led to his enlisting in the merchant marine two years later, when he was seventeen. Except for visits on leave, he hadn't been home to live since.

"Mindy tells me that you're a lawyer," he said, smiling slightly.

"That's right," Beth replied. "Surprised?"

Bram shook his head slowly, his eyes holding hers, and Beth felt a flush spreading up her neck.

"I knew you were one quick-smart lady," he said quietly, and Beth felt as if he had touched her.

"Brains and beauty, your Dad said to me," Bram went on. "And he was right. After you left, and I went back to sea, I discovered that I couldn't quite dismiss that combination, even in a teenage schoolgirl."

Beth held her breath, afraid to speak.

"The day after the barbecue, I told your father I was leaving anyway, there was no reason to ship you off to Boston," Bram said. "But he was convinced that you needed discipline, and boarding school was the answer. Just the thing to control a motherless girl."

"He thought I was a simpleton, a silly little flirt," Beth said bitterly.

"You were nothing like that," Bram said huskily.

"You just got mixed up with the wrong guy, on the wrong night."

Beth closed her eyes.

"Your father asked me not to contact you again, so I didn't, even though I knew he misunderstood it all. But after what happened, I thought it best to listen to him."

Mindy's voice sounded in the hall outside the door. They both started.

"My father didn't understand," Beth said helplessly.

"He couldn't," Bram replied. "I was sorry to hear of his death, Bethany. The news reached me six months after the funeral. I didn't get any mail until we docked in Iran."

"Beth? You in there?" Mindy called. She rapped on the door.

Bram dropped his eyes and walked back to the fireplace.

"Come in," Beth called.

Mindy entered, but stopped short when she saw Beth's companion.

"Melinda Sue," Bram greeted her. "I see your timing is still impeccable."

"Hello, Abraham," Mindy replied gravely, returning his formal address. "It didn't take you long to find Beth."

"Actually, she found me," Bram said, retrieving his glass from the mantel. "Don't let me put a damper on the festivities. I'll go and refill my empty glass." He brushed past Beth with a single electric glance and left the room.

Beth sank into the leather chair next to the fireplace.

"How did it go?" Mindy asked.

Beth couldn't reply.

"Is it still the same?" Mindy persisted.

Beth nodded dumbly, and then said, "It is for me."

"What did he say?" Mindy demanded.

Beth spread her hands. "A lot of things. You know how he talks, as if he were making fun of himself and everyone else at the same time. It's impossible to tell how much of what he says he really means."

"Some things never change," Mindy observed.

"He still hates Anabel and doesn't have much use for his father."

"Is he going to stay and run the show?"

"It sounds like it, but not out of any feeling of love. He seems to regard it as his duty."

Mindy shook her head wonderingly. "He's a difficult one to figure. Only Bram would turn his back on the most profitable tobacco concern in the Connecticut Valley to go off to sea. It's like Toby Tyler running away to join the circus."

"My father always suspected there was more to it than a desire on Bram's part to see the world."

"What do you mean?" Mindy asked, puzzled.

Beth stood again, running her fingers along the beveled edge of her father's desk. "Well, when Bram first left I was just a kid, but I used to hear him talking about it to my mother before she died. Dad always thought family problems drove Bram out the door."

"That's hardly news. Everybody knew that he and Anabel didn't get along once his father married her." Mindy's tone changed. "I'm sure it wasn't easy for Bram; he was a teenager and his father had a bride only a few years older than he was," she said sympathetically.

18

"Did you ever hear much about Bram's real mother?" Beth asked.

"No. He's supposed to look like her, though. Do you remember Jacinta, the housekeeper they had before Anabel let her go?"

"Of course. She went to school at night and she's a nurse at Johnson Memorial now."

"Right. Well, she knew the first Mrs. Curtis, and according to Jass she was a real beauty, dark like Bram, with skin like a camellia. That's a direct quote: *'como la camella'* is what she said."

"And is Anabel divorcing the old man now, or what?" Beth wanted to know.

Mindy shrugged. "That's anybody's guess. All I know is that she's gone. Hal says she's probably trying to stay married to Bram's father and outlast him. She'll get a bigger share of the estate that way."

Hal was Mindy's husband, a lawyer much given to voicing such opinions. He was a patent attorney for a Hartford corporation, however, so Beth would not be competing with him for private business.

"That reminds me," Mindy said. "Hal sent me to find you. Marion went upstairs to change and the groom needs help with the rest of the wedding presents."

Preoccupied with thoughts of Bram, Beth went with Mindy to supervise the distribution of the booty.

It was hours later, after the wedding couple had left and Beth was seeing the last stragglers out the door, when she encountered Bram again. She thought he'd gone home and, disappointed, had stopped looking for him. But just as she came back inside the house, he stepped from the shadows under the stairwell.

Beth froze, her eyes locked with his.

"I'm not going to bite you," Bram said quietly. "Don't look like that."

"How do I look?"

"Like a rabbit caught in the headlights of a car."

She hadn't realized that her reaction to him was so obvious. "I'm sorry," Beth said neutrally. "I was startled to see you. I thought that you had left."

"You mean you hoped that I had left," Bram amended.

Beth wasn't going to touch that, so she said instead, "I wish your father had been able to come with you today. Please give him my regards."

"I will. He's still confined to bed most of the time. He is recovering from the stroke, but progress is slow."

Having dispensed with the amenities, they stared at one another.

"Why are you still here?" Beth finally blurted out.

Bram laughed softly, an intensely intimate, masculine sound that transformed the silent hall. Beth began to wish fervently that some of the guests had stayed a little longer.

"I'm surprised law school didn't make you more diplomatic," Bram replied. "Aren't you supposed to learn subtlety there?"

"Sometimes I prefer the direct approach," Beth said coolly. "You didn't answer my question."

Bram pulled loose the knot of his tie and opened the top buttons of his collar. The casual gesture disturbed Beth inordinately, calling up images of the last time she had seen it. Then, he had taken off his shirt, and she had caressed him, unable to believe that he desired her. Beth Forsyth, coltish teenager, had changed into Bethany Forsyth, JD, but the searing memory remained, triggered by the innocent sensuality of his actions. Or maybe not so innocent, Beth thought. There was a sexual undertone to his demeanor with her that kept Beth constantly off balance, and she resented the advantage it gave him.

". . . wanted to see you again," he was saying.

"Why?"

"We were interrupted before, and there are some things I'd like to know."

Beth eyed him warily. "Such as?"

"Why haven't you gotten married?"

"I'm twenty-six, Bram, I think I have a little time left," Beth answered sarcastically. "And what makes you so sure I want to get married?"

"You must have had some offers," he said.

"A few. Is it any of your business?"

"I wondered why you didn't accept one of them."

Because I never could duplicate the experience I had with you, Beth thought. Aloud she said, "How do you know I'm not married? I've been away, I could have a husband somewhere. Female attorneys frequently keep their maiden names."

"You're not wearing a ring," Bram observed.

"So? Maybe I don't like to wear one." Why was she doing this? Simply because he was so sure of himself? Just once she would like to crack that smooth, charmingly detached facade. But perhaps she already had, just once, a long time ago.

He shook his head with deliberate conviction. "You would wear a ring," he said.

She faced him down, infuriated by his accurate

reading of her character. "It must be wonderful to know everything," she said tightly.

"Not everything. Just you."

Beth whirled away from him, confused. "What are you talking about? We had a few hours one night when you'd had too much to drink. From that you're able to deduce my views on life?" She wouldn't look at him.

"Sometimes you can tell more about a person from one night than you can tell about another person you see every day." His voice was low, controlled.

"That sounds like romantic nonsense," Beth replied crisply.

He moved to stand behind her. "That is undoubtedly the first time I've been accused of being a romantic," he said, amused.

This conversation was veering out of control. She shouldn't be talking like this with Bram; she was on the verge of revealing too much. Beth composed herself and turned to look at him.

"It's late," she said. "Shouldn't you be getting home?"

His dark eyes narrowed. "Are you throwing me out?" he inquired.

Beth caught her breath at the antagonism that flared in his face, in his tone. The hair-trigger temper that had been his trademark since childhood lay just beneath the surface, ready to explode with the right provocation. She wasn't going to supply it.

"Not at all," she answered evenly. "I know you're busy and I didn't want to keep you."

He snorted. "Busy with what?"

"Taking over Curtis Broadleaf. I'm sure you have a lot to do."

He sighed. "Oh, yes, I've been accepted back into the fold now that Daddy is flat on his back. He's turning me into quite the executive. I'm even thinking of joining the country club."

"That's the life you should have had all along, Bram," Beth said quietly.

"What if it's not the life I want!" he said fiercely, and then, seeing her alarmed reaction, he sighed and added wearily, "Never mind. I'll get lost while you tend to things here. I see the troops have left you with quite a mess."

"I have a crew coming in tomorrow morning to clean," Beth said.

"Admirable foresight," he commented.

Beth shot him a sidelong glance. Was he needling her again?

He knew what she was thinking and held up a hand. "I mean it. Anabel always sponsored mammoth debauches and then ran around screaming about the debris for days. Your way is much more efficient."

Beth couldn't resist the opening he'd provided. "How is Anabel?" she asked carefully.

"Dying, I hope. Or at least suffering from a debilitating disease."

The reply was so unexpected that Beth laughed. He apparently wasn't big on pleasantries.

"You find my viciousness amusing?" Bram asked, cocking his head.

"You're so outrageous, Bram. I know you don't mean that."

His lips twitched. "All right," he relented. "Maybe I don't wish her dead. But if I could lock her in a vault in Palm Beach, I would."

"Does your father miss her?"

"About as much as he would miss Typhoid Mary."

"He must have loved her once."

Bram's mouth thinned. "He was infatuated with her once."

"She was very pretty."

Bram inclined his head slowly, as if the admission were wrung from him. "Yes, she was."

"I'm glad she left so that you were able to come home," Beth said simply.

His head shot up, and his gaze became intent. "Why do you say that?"

Beth blinked, rattled. "Well, just because I know you two didn't get along."

He watched her a moment longer, and then nodded, satisfied. He walked past her to the door, stopping to lift a curl of dark brown hair from her neck.

"Good night, mouse," he said lightly, and left. Beth sagged against the door after she had closed it, blinking back tears.

Mouse. He had called her that the night her father found them together, after she'd told Bram she'd performed the part of a mouse in the school play.

It was so unfair of him to remember that, and use it on her like a weapon.

Her fists clenched. She didn't understand why after all this time Bram had finally acceded to his father's wishes and come home. It was clear he wasn't happy about his return, or the role his father wanted him to play, and Bram was the last person on earth who could be coerced into doing something against his will. He had always done exactly as he pleased. What was going on?

Beth straightened and walked through the house, ending up, as she had known she would, in her father's study. Unbidden, the memories washed over her again.

Bram had spoken of their time together with clarity, seeming to remember as much as Beth did. How could it have been that important to him? He was an experienced, well-traveled man. Beth didn't even want to think about the number of women he must have known during his seafaring days.

Beth settled in the chair next to the fireplace and stared at the picture of herself framed on her father's desk, lost in the past.

2

It was the fourth of July, three months before Beth's seventeenth birthday. Her father was hosting his annual barbecue for half the valley, and Beth had invited some of her schoolmates. All during the long summer afternoon they'd splashed in the pool and lounged around the patio, a small clutch of teenagers adrift in a sea of her father's friends. As the sun set in purple and orange splendor over the tobacco fields of northern Connecticut, Beth was ensconced in a deck chair by the diving board, sipping a soda. When she finished it Jim Hammond arrived and handed her another, which she took and sniffed warily. Beth had a strong suspicion Jim was trying to get her drunk. He considered himself to be her boyfriend, a subject on which they had a difference of opinion. Jim sat next to her, and Beth leaned forward to see past him to the crowd surrounding her father.

Carter Forsyth liked to entertain. A prominent accountant with a firm in Hartford, he opened his house to business and social acquaintances three or four times a year for gatherings like this one. He said that it helped to ease the loneliness created by his wife's death, and he might as well see his friends, because he would never remarry.

Beth knew that she was his main concern in life. Marion, her older sister, was home for the summer, but during the year she was away at college. Marion was a solid and sensible girl who would make a good marriage and settle down to respectability. But their father considered Beth to be another story. He saw rebellion in her individuality, and stubbornness in her determination to go her own way.

Feeling a pang of guilt, Beth got up and went over to her father, skirting the edge of the pool and walking barefoot onto the brick patio.

"Can I get you anything, Daddy?" she asked. "You've been looking after everyone else."

"No, thanks, honey," her father replied. "Just go into the garage and turn on the pool lights, if you would. It'll be getting dark soon."

As Beth turned to obey, she caught sight of a new arrival standing on the lawn. Deeply tanned, wearing jeans and a broadcloth shirt with the sleeves rolled above the elbows, a young man with dark, curly hair and a grin that flashed in the fading light stood talking to her sister. Instantly alert, Beth watched them for a moment and then backtracked to her father.

"Daddy, who is that?" she inquired, tugging on his sleeve.

Her father put aside his martini shaker and glanced at her. "Who?"

"That dark man, the one talking to Marion." Beth pointed surreptitiously.

Carter followed the direction of his daughter's hidden finger. "Oh. Why honey, don't you recognize him?"

Beth shook her head mutely. If she had seen him before, she would remember.

"I guess that's right," Carter said, "you were too young when he left. That's Bram Curtis, Joshua's son."

The name rang a bell, presenting a roll call of hair-raising stories associated with Mr. Curtis's sole offspring. Beth narrowed her eyes, trying to remember.

"I think he only came back to the house because Joshua and Anabel are away," Beth's father went on. "He never shows up when that woman is around. It's a damn shame. He's a wanderer on the face of the earth, that boy."

"Is he the one Momma used to talk about?" Beth asked.

Carter nodded. "She rather liked him."

It was coming back to Beth now. Her mother had always said that the Curtis boy had "gone to sea," in a wistful tone that suggested that she might have liked to go to sea herself. It was such a beautiful expression, calling up images of a sky filled with foreign constellations like the Southern Cross, and phosphorescent waves sparkling with St. Elmo's fire. Beth wanted to meet the man who had gone to sea.

"He sent me the kindest note when she died," Carter added. "I knew he was back at the house, so I called and asked him to come over today."

"That was nice, Daddy."

"Go and put those lights on for me, Beth," her father said.

Beth did as he asked, and when she got back Bram Curtis was gone. Marion still occupied the same spot, chatting with a middle-aged woman Beth didn't know.

Beth stifled her annoyance. It was just like her sister to let somebody like that get away. Marion might be three years her senior, but when it came to men she was as dense as a tree.

Beth waited until the older woman drifted away, and then corralled Marion.

"What happened to Bram Curtis?" she demanded.

Marion glanced at her, startled. "I don't know. What do you want with him?"

"I wanted to meet him."

"I'd watch out. He seems nice enough, but some of the things people say about him . . ." She shuddered delicately. "He scares me."

Beth sighed impatiently. Marion was afraid of everything. Scaring Marion was the highest recommendation Curtis could have; it proved beyond a shadow of a doubt that he wasn't in the same league with Marion's colorless college boyfriends, who put Beth to sleep.

"Did he go into the house?" Beth demanded.

Marion glanced around the lawn. "He might have, I

don't see him out here. He knows Mindy's family; he could have gone looking for her."

"Thanks, Marion, you've been a big help," Beth said sarcastically.

"Well, I'm not his bodyguard," Marion retorted. "And you'd better watch yourself; you know Daddy wouldn't like . . ."

Beth walked away, not staying to hear what Daddy wouldn't like. Daddy didn't like much of anything Beth did, and it had never stopped her.

Beth changed direction and slipped into the powder room just inside the door when she saw Jim heading her way. If she remained secluded long enough, maybe he would amuse himself elsewhere.

She looked into the mirror over the sink and assessed her reflection. Not bad, she thought, not half bad. Deep brown hair midway down her back, large blue eyes, pale skin lightly tanned for the summer, a mature figure encased in a two-piece bathing suit and a terry cover-up. She decided to go upstairs and change into something more appropriate for the evening, and peeked out the door to make sure the coast was clear.

Jim was gone. She made her way stealthily to the stairs, and was about to climb them when she glanced into the kitchen and saw the bottle of gin standing on the counter. It gave her an idea. She poured a glass of orange juice from the jug in the refrigerator. She was standing with the gin bottle in her hand, wondering how much liquor to add, when a masculine voice interrupted her thoughts.

"Aren't you a little young to be on the sauce?"

Beth jumped, almost dropping the liquor. Bram

Curtis stood in the doorway, lounging against the jamb, grinning at her.

"It's for my father," she answered guiltily.

"A likely story," he replied, laughing.

"I don't drink," she protested.

"Good for you, Beth. It is Beth, isn't it?"

"Yes."

"Short for Elizabeth?"

"Bethany."

"Bethany," he repeated, trying it out on his tongue. "Very pretty, like its owner. You must be driving all those adolescent males out of their minds."

Beth flushed. It was the sort of remark many people made, but the way he said it carried an implication beyond the compliment. She could see immediately why he unnerved Marion. But Beth was not her sister; what intimidated the older girl intrigued the younger. Beth moved closer, looking at him.

"I seem to remember a first-grader who was never seen without a mangy mutt with a scraggly gray tail, and a giant lollipop," Bram said. "I must say you've made a splendid progression from all-day suckers."

"The dog was Alcatraz," Beth replied. "He went into convulsions last winter and we had to put him to sleep."

Bram's dark eyes filled with sympathy. "I'm sorry," he said. "That must have been very hard for you."

Why, he's nice, Beth thought suddenly. She felt a surge of confidence. "It was," she replied. "I had him since I was two."

Bram came into the kitchen and took the glass from Beth's hand. "Why don't we forget this, and you can

31

come and talk to me. Tell me all about high school. I have a burning desire to relive the days of my ill-spent youth."

Beth giggled. He was a wonderful talker; it was a treat to listen to him.

"Okay," she agreed eagerly, even though she suspected his idea had more to do with keeping her away from the gin than his curiosity about her life. But one look into his liquid brown eyes convinced her that it didn't matter; she wanted to be with him, and that was it.

"Where shall we go?" he asked, looking around.

"My father's study?"

He made a sweeping gesture with his glass. "Lead on, fair lady."

Bram followed Beth down the hall to the den while she wondered why he was choosing to spend time with her. Surely he had better things to do. Then he smiled down at her as she opened the door, and she ceased to care whether he was trying to maintain her sobriety or gathering material for an exposé on her nonexistent love life. She shut the door after them and sat down.

"Now," he said, "what's new at Suffield High?"

He was sitting in her father's leather chair, leaning forward, his elbows on his knees. The overhead lighting cast shadows along the planes of his face and emphasized his high cheekbones. His black hair curled over his forehead and down to the nape of his neck. His eyelashes were long, sweeping his lower lids when he glanced down. Dark hair grew along his forearms and escaped from the vee of his shirt at the neck. He smiled, and his teeth shone white against his dusky

You know the thrill of escaping to a world of PASSION...SENSUALITY ...DESIRE...SEDUCTION... and LOVE FULFILLED...

Escape again... with 4 FREE novels and

get more great Silhouette Desire novels —for a 15-day FREE examination— delivered to your door every month!

Silhouette Desire offers you real-life drama and romance of successful women in charge of their lives and their careers, women who face the challenges of today's world to make their dreams come true. They are not for everyone, they're for women who want a sensual, provocative reading experience.

These are modern love stories that begin where other romances leave off. They take you *beyond* the others and into a world of love fulfilled and passions realized. You'll share precious, private moments and secret dreams...experience every whispered word of love, every ardent touch, every passionate heartbeat. And now you can enter the unforgettable world of Silhouette Desire romances each and every month.

FREE BOOKS

You can start today by taking advantage of this special offer— the 4 newest Silhouette Desire

romances (a $9.00 Value) *absolutely FREE,* along with a Mystery Gift. Just fill out and mail the attached postage-paid order card.

AT-HOME PREVIEWS
FREE DELIVERY

After you receive your 4 free books and Mystery Gift, every month you'll have the chance to preview more Silhouette Desire romances—*before they're available in stores!* When you decide to keep them, you'll pay just $11.70 (a $13.50 Value), *with no additional charges of any kind and no risk!* You can cancel your subscription at any time just by dropping us a note. In any case, the first 4 books and Mystery Gift are yours to keep.

EXTRA BONUS

When you take advantage of this offer, we'll also send you the Silhouette Books Newsletter free with every shipment. Every informative issue features news on upcoming titles, interviews with your favorite authors, and even their favorite recipes.

Get a Free
Mystery Gift, too!

**EVERY BOOK YOU RECEIVE WILL BE
A BRAND-NEW FULL-LENGTH NOVEL!**

CLIP AND MAIL THIS POSTPAID CARD TODAY!

NO POSTAGE
NECESSARY
IF MAILED
IN THE
UNITED STATES

BUSINESS REPLY CARD
FIRST CLASS PERMIT NO. 194 CLIFTON, N.J.

Postage will be paid by addressee

**Silhouette Books
120 Brighton Road
P.O. Box 5084
Clifton, NJ 07015-9956**

Escape with 4 Silhouette Desire novels (a $9.00 Value) and get a Mystery Gift, too!

Silhouette Desire®

Silhouette Books, 120 Brighton Rd., P.O. Box 5084, Clifton, NJ 07015-9956

Yes, please send me FREE and without obligation, the 4 newest Silhouette Desire novels along with my Mystery Gift. Unless you hear from me after I receive my 4 FREE books, please send me 6 new Silhouette Desire novels soon as they are published. I understand that you will bill me a total of just $11.70 (a $13.50 Value), with no additional charges of any kind. There is no minimum number of books that I must buy, and I can cancel at any time. The first 4 books and Mystery Gift are mine to keep, even if I never take a single additional book.

NAME _____
(please print)

ADDRESS _____

CITY _____ STATE _____ ZIP _____

SIGNATURE (If under 18, parent or guardian must sign).

Terms and prices subject to change. Your enrollment is subject to acceptance by Silhouette Books.

SILHOUETTE DESIRE and colophon are registered trademarks.

CTD 725

skin. Beth swallowed. She had never seen a man like this one; he looked like an oil painting of a sixteenth-century explorer, or the carving on a Medici tomb.

"You're staring at me," he admonished softly.

"Sorry," Beth mumbled, mortified. "My father told me about you, and I guess I'm curious."

"Uh oh," he said, swirling the ice in his glass. "Don't tell me that my deplorable reputation has preceded me. You know who I am, then?"

Beth nodded. "And I've heard something about the ill-spent youth you mentioned."

His eyes roamed the walls. "I was hoping to remain anonymous a little longer. I didn't want to frighten you away."

"I'm not frightened," Beth said quickly.

He smiled slightly. "I see that you're not. Anyway, don't believe everything you hear."

"My father didn't say anything bad about you. He just said you couldn't get along with your stepmother and that it had made you a wanderer on the face of the earth."

Bram thought that over. "It always amazes me that I find support in the most unlikely places," he said musingly.

"I remember my mother told me that when they threw you off the football team you punched the coach and knocked him out."

He looked at the ceiling. "That," he said gravely, "was not my finest hour."

"It made sense to me," Beth replied fervently. "I've wanted to deck my gym teacher plenty of times."

He shook his head. "You look too smart to indulge in that kind of childish behavior. I was full of pain in

33

those days, or even I wouldn't have done something so immature."

"Why were you full of pain?" Beth asked ingenuously.

He looked sharply at her. "You have quite a facility for getting me to talk. I thought the subject was going to be you."

"Dull subject," Beth said gloomily.

"I disagree. What have you been up to at school?"

She thought about it. "I was a mouse in the school play last year," she offered.

He looked startled. "A mouse?"

"Yeah, in the *Nutcracker Suite*. I was in the mouse chorus in the scene around the Christmas tree. I was one of the dancing mice."

He grinned. "Someone must have made a mistake. You're much too vivid to be cast as a mouse."

"And I won the Latin prize last June," Beth added.

"What did you win?"

"A framed certificate and a Latin dictionary," she said unhappily.

"Not exactly what you had in mind?" he suggested.

"No," she admitted. She brightened. "Would you like to hear some Latin?"

"Hit me," he said, draining his glass.

"'*In hoc signo vinces,*'" she recited.

"Very impressive. What does it mean?"

"'In this sign thou shalt conquer.' The Emperor Constantine saw it written in the sky the night before his big battle, I forget what it was. Do you want to hear some more?"

"By all means. Toss me another one."

"'*Dulce et decorum est pro . . .*'"

"'*patri mori,*'" Bram finished for her.

"You know it?" Beth asked, delighted. "You know Latin?"

"No, but I read. I read a lot. You spend quite a bit of time alone on a ship, and it passes the hours. That means, as I recall, 'It is a sweet and beautiful thing to die for one's country.'"

"Right!" Beth said, pleased.

Bram got up and poured several fingers of liquor into his glass from the bottle Beth's father kept on his desk. "Do you think he'll mind?" he asked Beth.

"No, go ahead," she said, watching Bram. He seemed to be drinking a lot.

He sat again. "Go on, go on," he said, waving his hand. "Tell me more."

Beth didn't need much encouragement. She launched into a spirited monologue about her life and times, which soon had him laughing and offering amusing comments. They talked until Bram caught Beth glancing at the clock on the wall. They'd been in the den for three hours!

Bram rose. "I'm keeping you from your guests," he said quickly. "I mustn't be so selfish." He moved to leave.

Beth jumped up, too. "No, don't go," she said anxiously. "Please stay with me."

He halted, looking at her with a measuring glance. "All right," he agreed. "But let me get you something to eat. I've had you in here all night."

"Fine," she replied, ready to agree to anything that would keep him with her.

"What would you like?" he asked.

Anything, anything. "A hot dog, I guess; I can smell them cooking. And a drink."

"Coming up," he said, heading for the door.

"You'll come back?" she asked worriedly.

"Of course," he replied gently. "In a flash. Don't let anybody take my place."

As if anyone could, Beth thought. She followed him into the hall, fidgeting, and ran into Mindy Crawford, her best friend.

"Where have you been?" Mindy asked. "Jim has been looking all over for you."

"Mindy, don't tell him you've seen me. I'm hoping he'll just go home."

"What's going on? This place isn't that big; you can't dodge him forever."

"Tell him I felt sick and went to bed."

"Beth! You can't do that. This is your house. You're the hostess."

"My father is the host. I'm the pain-in-the-neck kid."

Mindy opened her mouth to speak, and then stopped at the sound of Jim's voice behind them. Beth slipped back into the den, but it was too late. He'd seen her, and Mindy shot her a sympathetic glance as she left.

"I thought you'd taken off," Jim greeted her.

"I've been around," Beth said evenly.

"Have you been avoiding me?" he asked belligerently.

"I can't help it if you think so," Beth said, turning away.

"Hey, wait a minute," Jim said, grabbing her arm. "What's this disappearing act? You're supposed to be my girl."

"Only in your mind," Beth replied stiffly. He was still holding her, and as she tried to shrug free he tightened his grip.

"Let me go," she said fiercely.

"So you can vanish again? I will not. You've been acting pretty weird lately, Beth, and I think I deserve an explanation."

"I don't have to explain anything to you. Let me go!"

Jim's hand enclosed her arm like a vise. Tears sprang to her eyes. He was stronger than he looked. She struggled silently.

"Back off, sonny," Bram's voice said.

Jim spun around. "Who are you?"

"Does it matter?" Bram said pleasantly. "I'm the guy who's telling you to let her go, and I'm bigger than you are."

Jim released Beth, shooting her a furious glance. He brushed past Bram, heading for the sliding doors to the patio.

Bram pushed open the study door with his shoulder and set the plate and glass he was carrying on the desk. "Friend of yours?" he asked mildly.

"He's a pest," Beth replied, rubbing her arm. Her face was white with shock.

Bram noticed her expression. "Hey, take it easy. Did he rattle you?"

Beth blinked rapidly. "I guess so. He was really hurting me."

Bram opened his arms. "Come here, *mouse*. Erase that memory with me."

Beth ran to him, snuggling against his broad chest. He held her tightly, smoothing her hair.

"Better?" he asked gently.

"Yes," she whispered.

He moved to let her go, and she clung. "Hold me," she begged. "Just a little longer."

He complied, enfolding her again. Beth closed her eyes and relaxed against him. She had never been held by a man, only by inexperienced boys who grabbed her awkwardly and didn't know where to put their hands. Bram held her easily, with the confidence of long practice.

"Look at that moon," Beth murmured dreamily, seeing it through the window over his shoulder. "When it's full like that you can see all the craters."

"That's a reckless moon," Bram said, a smile in his voice. "That's what an old sea dog I shipped out with once used to call it. A moon like that makes you do things you wouldn't do otherwise. It makes you foolish."

Beth sighed, burrowing into his shoulder. He smelled good, clean and fresh, an impression enhanced by the starch in his shirt. His body was hard and firm where she touched him. She felt languid, dreamy, but had a heightened awareness of Bram's maleness at the same time.

"Come on, mousie," Bram said, holding her at arm's length. "Eat your dinner before it gets cold."

"I'm not hungry," Beth said, looking up at him.

As he gazed down at her, his expression seemed to change. The amusement left his face and was replaced by a dawning realization of their closeness, and her response to him. Slowly, he bent and pressed his lips to hers.

Beth kissed him back eagerly, unsure of what she was doing, but guided by a rush of desire such as she had never felt before in her life. Bram had meant to kiss her briefly, sweetly, but when he felt her lips opening under his, her slender, curved body pressing into him, he forgot her age, her father, and everything else. This was a lovely woman who wanted him, and he was not used to declining such invitations.

Beth wound her arms around his neck, afraid that he might pull away at any second. She knew instinctively that the way to hold him was to carry him into deep waters fast, where he would be too involved to break the embrace. She grew bolder, caressing him, and his gasp of pleasure was her reward.

"Baby, you don't know what you're doing," he whispered hoarsely, lifting his mouth from hers.

"Teach me," she responded. "Teach me everything I need to know."

He groaned and pulled at the collar of her terry robe. As he kissed her neck and exposed shoulder, Beth could smell the liquor on his breath, faint and acerbic. He wouldn't make love to me if he were cold sober, she thought fleetingly, and then pushed the idea away. She didn't care. He was the most exciting man she'd ever met, and his kisses drove the sloppy pawings of her high-school beaux from her mind.

His mouth returned to hers, urgently, and he bent to pick her up, carrying her the few steps to the divan near the door. He set her down gently and then dropped next to her, cradling her against him. Beth lay back and watched him, silently, as he unbelted her short terry robe and discarded it, moving immediately to kiss her breasts, covered only by the bra top of her bathing suit. His lips traveled over the soft flesh, and Beth arched her back, whimpering and holding his head, tangling her fingers in his thick hair. When he reached for the catch at the back of her top, she lifted herself to accommodate him. He pulled it from her and dropped it on the floor.

"Beautiful," he murmured. "So beautiful." He

gathered her to him, pressing his mouth to the valley between her breasts, where Beth had never felt the touch of a man's lips. She sighed and closed her eyes. He moved, teasing first one nipple and then the other with his tongue. Beth shuddered delicately, unable to look, unable to speak, certain only that she wanted this miracle to continue.

Bram sat up, undoing his shirt quickly with one hand, impatiently. He pulled it off with one swift gesture, and he was back with her in a second, descending to Beth's welcoming arms.

The shock of his bare flesh excited her, and Beth kissed his chest, running her hands over his smooth shoulders, lifting her mouth for the return of his. She thought he wouldn't stop now; he was sure, purposeful, accustomed to carrying these preliminaries to their logical conclusion. But when he reached for her briefs, he seemed to step back for a moment and realize what was happening.

"I can't do this," he muttered, withdrawing his hand. "It isn't right."

Beth pressed his big hand with her small one, clinging to him. "Yes, it is," she protested. "I've never felt this way before, Bram. This is what all the songs and poems are about. It must be right."

Bram's face shadowed with concern. "Wait, Beth, listen to me . . ."

Beth answered him with a kiss, showing him what she'd learned in his arms, and his scruples vanished in the heat of passion. "I'll lock the door," he murmured against her mouth, and at the same instant the door opened and Beth's father walked through it.

Beth would never forget the look on his face as he took in the two of them prone on the couch, half naked, their discarded clothes in a heap on the floor. Carter Forsyth's eyes widened in shock. Then he assumed a carefully blank expression and turned his back.

"Bethany, dress yourself," he directed in a quiet voice.

Bram leaped to his feet, handing Beth her robe and placing himself between her and her father, as if to protect her from attack. "This isn't Beth's fault, sir," he said quickly. "I'm responsible."

Beth's father turned back to face them. "I know that," he said coldly to Bram. "But my daughter had to offer you some encouragement. This doesn't look like rape to me."

"Wait," Bram began, but Beth's father held up his hand to forestall argument. Beth, belting her robe, could see Bram decide that he would only make the situation worse by contradicting Carter Forsyth.

"I want you to leave this house," Beth's father said to Bram. "I am bitterly disappointed in you, Curtis. I invited you here, and this is how you take advantage of my hospitality. It seems my late wife's affection for you was misplaced. I never put much stock in what was said about you, but it now appears that I should have listened."

"Daddy, that isn't fair," Beth protested, but Bram reached back to squeeze her arm, silencing her.

"I'll go," Bram said to her father, his mouth tight with some unnamed emotion. "But I want to talk to Beth first. Alone."

"Absolutely not," Carter fumed, reddening.

"I insist," Bram said in a low tone that indicated he meant it.

Carter blinked, and then, to Beth's amazement,

nodded. She had never seen him back down to anyone before.

"I'll be right outside the door," he said in parting.

Bram turned to Beth immediately and enfolded her in his arms.

"Mouse, I'm sorry," he whispered. "I am so sorry."

Beth burrowed into him, drawing sustenance from his strength.

"Beth, listen to me," he went on. "You are not to blame for this. I led you into it. I should be shot for putting you in this position."

Beth didn't answer, her horror at her father's reaction fading in the warmth and security of Bram's embrace.

"I don't want you to feel guilty about this. Do you understand?" He held her off to look into her face.

Beth nodded, lost in his eyes.

He pulled her close again, stroking her hair. "Oh, baby, listen to me. Don't let your father make you feel ashamed. Your feelings are normal and healthy and one day you're going to be a fantastic lover for some lucky man."

"I wanted him to be you," Beth murmured against his shoulder.

She felt his lips in her hair. "No, no. I'm glad in a way that your father came in when he did. He stopped something I shouldn't have started. But that doesn't mean it won't be wonderful for you some time in the future with a man you love."

"I love you," she said. "It can happen this fast, I know it can."

He went still, and then his arms tightened. "Beth," he said, a catch in his voice. "How young you are, and how fresh. I'd give anything to regain the innocence you're so eager to lose." He pried her arms loose from his neck and tilted her chin with his hand, forcing her to look at him.

"Beth, I have to go. I don't want to, but I can't damage your relationship with your father any more. Are you going to be all right?"

"Yes," she replied. "But won't I see you again, can't I write to you?"

He shook his head. "It's best to let it go." He smiled charmingly, and her heart turned over. "I'm too old for you, you know."

"I'll hurry if you'll wait."

He closed his eyes, and Beth saw his indecision. But then he opened them, and she realized that this time good judgment had triumphed over emotion. He wasn't going to make the same mistake twice in one night.

"No, mouse. I'm trouble for you. Haven't I proved it?"

"I don't care if you're trouble for me."

"Well, I do. You're a nice girl and you should steer clear of a guy like me." He eyed her intently "Be brave, now."

Beth smiled shakily and straightened her shoulders.

"Good girl." Bram ran his fingertip down her nose. "I think it will be very difficult to forget you," he said grimly, "but for your sweet sake I am going to try."

Beth's eyes filled. She hadn't cried at her father's outrage, but the thought of Bram leaving reduced her to tears.

Bram touched her cheek, and a hot droplet splashed on his hand.

"Good-bye, mouse," he said, and kissed her lips lightly. Then he picked up his shirt, shrugged into it, and was gone.

Beth sank into a chair, drained.

After a few moments she became aware of the sound of low, male voices outside the door. Her father and Bram, probably. She didn't want to think about it.

Time passed, and she didn't move until the door opened and Mindy entered, her eyes wide.

"What's going on?" she asked in hushed tones. "I saw your father and Bram Curtis talking in the hall, and your father looked wild. Did you meet him, by the way, Bram, I mean? Isn't he the most wickedly attractive man? He was at our house the other night, and I practically sprained myself trying to get him to notice me, but he spent the whole time talking to my father about tobacco blight, or some damn thing. . . ."

Mindy trailed off as she realized Beth wasn't listening to her.

"Beth. What's the matter? Did something happen?"

Beth sighed. Mindy would plague her until she answered her question, so she gave her friend an abbreviated version of the evening's events.

Mindy whistled at the conclusion. "Bram Curtis! You lucky dog!" Then her expression changed as she considered the other aspect of the situation. "Your father is going to kill you."

Beth threw her a dirty look. "Get out of here, Mindy," she said. "My dad will be back in a minute, and I don't want you to get caught in the crossfire."

Mindy needed no further encouragement. "Call me tomorrow," she said over her shoulder, and left Beth alone.

A few minutes later the door opened again to admit

Carter Forsyth, and Beth steeled herself to deal with the results of her interlude with Bram. Her father announced that she would leave for boarding school immediately. Even though it was the middle of the summer, Carter knew a school that kept open a wing of the dormitory for foreign students who lived on campus year-round, and Beth could be installed there in a matter of days.

Beth saw no reason to contest the plan. She wanted to get away from her father; she knew that after this incident his restrictions would be even more oppressive than ever. A change might do them both good.

And until the night of Marion's reception, she never saw Bram again.

3

꧁⋄⋄⋄⋄⋄⋄⋄⋄⋄⋄꧂

The next morning, Beth was awakened by the sound of the doorbell. The cleaning crew had arrived. She left them to their work and went upstairs to shower and change.

When she came back down the house was beginning to resemble its former status, and she went down the lane to get the mail. Her mouth went dry when she saw that it contained an eggshell-colored vellum envelope from the Connecticut State Bar Association. She ripped it open quickly, scanned the first few lines, and then let out a whoop of glee. She had passed the bar exam and was now admitted to practice law in the state.

She looked around excitedly, and then experienced the deflation common to all those who receive good news alone: There was no one to tell. She ran inside to call Mindy, and as she approached the phone, it rang.

"Hello?" she said excitedly, her attention still focused on the letter in her hand.

"Hi," Bram's voice said, and the folded sheet slipped through her fingers. "I was wondering if you'd like to have dinner with me."

Beth stared at the tile floor, wracked by indecision. She wanted to go more than anything, but last night had taught her that Bram still exercised the same fascination, still had the power to hurt her and turn her life upside down. If she was going to live here and work here, it would be best to avoid him.

"I don't think so, Bram," she heard herself saying stiffly, and then winced at the starkness of her reply.

There was a silence, and then a short bark of laughter. "I see that the passage of time has managed to tarnish the brightness of my appeal."

Hardly that, Beth thought. "I'm busy," she added lamely.

She could hear his sigh over the line. "Maybe you'll change your mind if I tell you it isn't entirely a social occasion. The fact is, I need a lawyer, and I thought you might be willing to represent the company."

Beth bit her lip. He certainly knew how to make things difficult. Curtis Broadleaf generated a lot of legal work, and she would be an idiot to turn him down.

"Of course," he went on, "if you're booked too solid to take on any clients. . . ."

Beth made a wry face at the receiver. He knew she was just getting started. What a schemer he was; she was almost tempted to tell him to take his business elsewhere.

"What about Don Matheson?" Beth asked, naming the lawyer who had always handled Bram's father's affairs.

"I've been going over the books, and I'm not too satisfied with the way he's been handling things," Bram answered.

Beth was silent, hesitating.

"Did I hurt you so badly that you won't even see me in a professional capacity?" Bram asked quietly.

"Where do you want to go?" Beth inquired, accepting the challenge he'd offered by taking such a personal tack. She would show him that she could deal with him on a business level; he wasn't going to get her to admit that there was anything more involved.

"How about the Signature?" Bram asked. It was a downtown Hartford restaurant, located in the Civic Center, a bit fancy for discussion purposes, but Beth didn't feel like debating the point.

"All right," she agreed.

"What time shall I pick you up?"

"I'll meet you there," Beth responded quickly. She didn't want this to take on the semblance of a date. "About seven-thirty, okay?"

"Fine," Bram answered, his neutral tone revealing nothing.

"Bring along any information you think might be pertinent," Beth added, to enhance the professional flavor of the encounter.

"Right, counselor," Bram said abruptly. "See you then." The line went dead.

Beth took a lot of time deciding what to wear that night. She told herself that it was just another dinner meeting with a client, and she had had enough of those while she was working as an intern at a Boston legal firm. But this client was Bram, and she wavered between a steadfast refusal to dress for him and the temptation to select her most flattering outfit and look her best. To her own disgust vanity won, and she emerged from her bedroom at seven o'clock dressed in a royal-blue silk shirtwaist that enhanced her eyes and the creamy blush on her light skin. Her hair was pulled back into a topknot and then cascaded to her shoulders, revealing pearl earrings. A camel bag and matching sling-back pumps completed the ensemble, and while Beth knew she wasn't overdressed for the occasion, she also knew that she had devoted more care to her toilette than usual. She shrugged lightly as she made her way outside to her car. She wasn't sixteen anymore, and her father wasn't going to punish her for displaying an interest in the black sheep of the Curtis family. She was on her own.

The drive to Hartford took about twenty-five minutes, and she was right on time as she approached the attendant inside the lounge of the restaurant.

"I'm meeting Mr. Curtis," she said, and was led to a table for two by the window. Bram rose at her approach.

He was dressed in a charcoal-gray lightweight jacket that called attention to his dark good looks, with pants of a lighter gray and an off-white shirt with a navy tie. The lamplight reflected the sheen of his gleaming black hair and the glint of his gold cufflinks. Beth looked around nervously. The atmosphere was a little too subdued and romantic for her comfort.

"You look very pretty," Bram said as he pulled out her chair.

"Thank you," she said properly, a grade-schooler reacting politely to a teacher's praise.

Bram didn't miss the implication of her tone, and as if to demonstrate that his motives were exactly as represented, he put a file on the table in front of her the minute she was seated.

"Take a look at that," he said, "and tell me if you think that Matheson has been giving my father's company short shrift."

Bram summoned the steward and ordered wine while Beth perused the file. After she had read the documents and asked Bram some pertinent questions she had to admit that she agreed with him.

"Will you take the account then?" Bram asked.

The waiter appeared to take their order, and after he left Bram eyed her expectantly. "Well?" he persisted.

Beth took a sip of the Chablis Bram had selected, and discovered that it was very good.

"I feel I should tell you that I've never done this type of work before," Beth hedged. "The firm I clerked for handled mostly wills and divorces, that type of thing."

"But you could do it, couldn't you? With some research?"

"Yes, I suppose so," Beth replied warily.

"Your enthusiasm is overwhelming," Bram said sarcastically. He reached over and closed the file in front of Beth, pulling it to his side of the table. "Forget it. I'm sorry I bothered you."

Beth looked down at her linen napkin, saying nothing.

"You certainly have turned into the citadel of caution, haven't you?" he went on acerbically. "Whatever happened to that enchanting teenager who grabbed for life with both hands?"

"I grew up and left her behind," Beth replied slowly.

He shook his head. "No, I think you buried her under an avalanche of law books and suspicion. She's still there, but she needs to be coaxed out of her hiding place."

Beth raised her blue eyes to his brown ones. "By whom?" she asked softly.

"By me," he replied, "if you'll give me the chance."

Beth stood, her purse sliding from her lap and hitting the floor. "You had your chance," she said abruptly, and turned from the table, almost colliding with the astonished waiter, who dodged her nimbly, balancing their tray of food. Beth bent and retrieved her bag, heading for the door.

Bram caught up to her in the lobby, seizing her arm and spinning her around to face him. "Beth, wait," he said, his face anxious.

"No," she whispered, her eyes filming over with tears. "I won't wait. I waited for you for ten years, and I'm not going to wait any more."

Bram's hands fell away, and Beth fled, blinking rapidly to clear her vision. All she could think about was getting away from him and back home.

But when she arrived there Bram was waiting for her, seated in his father's long black Buick. He jumped out of it the minute she pulled into the driveway.

"How did you beat me back here?" she asked in amazement, her surprise at his feat momentarily sublimating her other feelings.

"I drove seventy all the way," he said grimly, "because I was afraid you wouldn't let me into the house if you got here first."

They stared at one another.

"We have to talk," Bram finally said. "You can dodge me until you're exhausted with it, but I'll run you to earth eventually. You know I will."

Beth nodded wearily. He was nothing if not persistent. She led the way to the front door and unlocked it.

Once inside, they went to the living room, and Beth sat in a wing chair next to the big bay window. "Help yourself," she said, gesturing to the bar against the wall.

Bram quickly made a drink, and then sat opposite Beth after she declined his offer to mix something for her. She should have accepted, she thought as soon as the words were out of her mouth; she was so tense that her knuckles were white where she clutched the arms of the chair.

"What did you mean about waiting for me for ten years?" Bram asked, plunging right back into the depths again.

"Think hard, sailor," Beth replied bitterly. "Maybe you can figure it out."

He took a healthy slug of his bourbon. "I take it you're referring to the night of your father's party."

"Bingo."

"Was it so important to you?" he asked carefully, watching her face.

"A lot more important than it was to you," Beth

answered, getting up and walking to the other side of the room. "You obviously dismissed it, and me, the minute you left the party."

"I never said that."

"You never said anything!" Beth cried, whirling to face him. "You walked out of my father's house, this house, and that was the end of it."

"Your father wanted it that way," Bram said.

"My father!" Beth answered incredulously. "Don't make me laugh. You would never let him or anybody else stand in the way of what you wanted. Which only leads me to one conclusion. You didn't want me."

Bram stood also, pacing. "That isn't true. I wanted you very much. And if you can't accept that, your recollection of that evening isn't as clear as mine."

Beth held up her hand. "Excuse me, you're right. You wanted me physically, I remember that very well. What you didn't want was a relationship with a clinging teenager who would foul up your plans to have a girl in every port."

His eyes widened. "Is that what you think? That I let you go because I had to answer the call of the sirens or some stupid notion?"

Beth fell silent, halted by the derision in his voice. She had believed her version of the story so long that his contradiction confused her. "Isn't that right?" she finally asked.

Bram closed his eyes, putting his empty glass on the coffee table. It was some seconds before he spoke again. "Beth, listen to me. You were sixteen years old. You were the sweetest, truest thing that had ever happened to me, and I couldn't spoil you. It was hard for me to leave, harder still to let you grow up and live your life without hearing from me. But I know I did what was best, Beth. I was no good for you. You needed a chance to get an education, meet people, develop into the person you are today. Believe me when I tell you that walking away from you that night was the noblest thing I've ever done in my singularly ignoble life."

"Are you saying my father was right?"

"He was right about my unsuitability for you at that time."

She stared at him in dumb disbelief, then shook her head. "The two of you, so wise, so knowing, so *male*, deciding what was best for me. What about what I wanted?"

Bram looked back at her, unmoving.

"I tried to get your address from everybody who knew you after you left," she said quietly. "Nobody could tell me where you were. Then I told myself that surely you would call me, contact me when I was home from school, get my dorm address from Mindy, do something. But when the days passed and then the weeks and the months I finally realized that I was just an evening's diversion for you."

Bram's fist slammed into the wall behind him. "Haven't you been listening to a word I've been saying?"

"Oh, yes, I heard. A touching story, full of kindness and self-sacrifice. But didn't you leave something out?"

Bram watched her, his brown eyes intent.

"I scared you, didn't I?" she went on softly. "You knew that it couldn't be one night and then good-bye forever with me, you sized up the situation very well. I was a kid and kids don't understand about mature relationships that allow for sex but bypass commitment and what it implies. I wanted it all, and you weren't ready to give it."

Bram dropped his eyes, and she saw that she had struck a nerve.

"And why didn't you contact me later, when I was older and had acquired some of the experience you seemed to think was so important? I've had years to figure it all out; you still weren't ready for the kind of relationship I wanted. And you aren't now."

He said nothing.

"What made you so cynical, Bram? Who convinced you that women aren't to be trusted?"

He glared at her stonily, but didn't answer.

"Was it Anabel?" she asked suddenly, on a hunch.

His reaction betrayed him. His mouth thinned and his eyes became as hard as flint at the mention of his stepmother's name.

"Leave her out of this," he snarled.

"What did she do?"

"I said to drop it. She has nothing to do with me and you."

"I think she does. Why did you leave home to get away from her? Was she so intolerable?"

"I'm not on the witness stand," Bram countered. "Don't try to cross-examine me."

"I wish I did have you on the witness stand," Beth said fervently. "I'd get the truth out of you."

"The truth is no mystery," Bram said, looking away from her. "My mother died and my father married somebody I didn't like. It happens every day. Don't you watch television?"

Beth shook her head. "There's more to it than that."

Bram's brow darkened furiously. "Stop probing!

God, you're infuriating. Is this what college did for you? I liked you better at sixteen."

"When I believed everything you told me?" Beth inquired archly.

His fists clenched, but he didn't respond.

"I believed it all," Beth repeated. "And remembered it. Shall I recite it for you now?"

"Beth . . ." Bram said warningly.

"Let's see," Beth went on musingly. "Something about my not being ashamed of what had happened between us because my feelings were natural and normal. Wasn't that it?"

He took a step toward her, his eyes blazing.

"And oh yes, someday I would be a wonderful lover for some lucky man. Have I got it right?"

The fingers of his right hand flexed.

"Go ahead and punch me," Beth cried. "That's what you usually do when somebody makes you angry, isn't it? Don't hold back on my account."

He reached out for her, and she struggled. Without hurting her he managed to subdue her and pull her into his arms.

"I don't want to punch you, I want to make love to you," he murmured, tangling his fingers in her trailing hair and turning her face up to his. "I've wanted nothing else since I saw you at your sister's reception."

Beth tried to hang on to the last vestiges of her pride, her resistance, but they were slipping rapidly out of reach. This was Bram, and he was touching her, holding her. Other concerns just didn't seem to matter.

"We've waited so long to be together again," he said huskily. "Let's not fight." His lips brushed her cheek.

Beth's head turned involuntarily to bring her mouth to his. He kissed her gently at first, her awareness distracted slightly by the unfamiliar, tactile softness of his mustache, his beard. But then, as the pressure of Bram's lips increased, she was submerged in a rush of sensual memory so intense her knees went weak and she dug her nails into his arms for support. After all this time, she thought dizzily, how can it still be so strong? She didn't understand the basis of an attraction that could endure with such force, without contact, for such a long period. All she knew was that for ten years, through every experience of her life, she had never met a man who could make her feel what Bram was making her feel now.

He lifted his mouth from hers and kissed her neck, brushing her hair away from her ear and whispering into it, "Do you want to go upstairs?"

When Beth hesitated he bent his head and trailed his lips inside the collar of her dress, kissing her collarbone. He dropped his hands to her hips and pulled her tight against him, letting her feel his arousal. Beth gasped and went limp in his arms. Bram held her gently for a moment, as if to reassure her, and then turned her toward the stairs.

The movement released Beth from her trance. I can't let this happen, she thought wildly. He doesn't love me; if I go with him I will be no different from all the others. Bram was special to her, he always would be, and if she couldn't be special to him, she would be nothing at all.

"No," she said suddenly, clearly, and Bram stopped dead.

He grasped her shoulders and stared into her face. "What?"

"I said no. I can't do this."

"Beth, why not? You want me. That's one thing that has never changed."

"I didn't say I didn't want you. But I needed more when I was sixteen, and I still do. You can give me your body, Bram, but I want you to give yourself. Until you're ready to do that please don't tempt me with glimpses of something that just can't be."

He was silent, his expression shrouded, and then he released her. "All right," he said finally. "I'll go. But it could have been very good for us."

Beth's breath caught in her throat. She had no doubt of that. Her heart was still racing from her short time in his embrace.

"I'm sure it's been good for you with a lot of women," Beth replied, her voice unsteady.

He smiled faintly. "Stubborn as always, I see," he said softly.

Her chin came up slightly. "I hold out for what I want, Bram. If that makes me stubborn, then I guess I am." She touched his cheek, and his eyes closed. "You were my first taste of love, Abraham Curtis, and I've always wanted to have the rest. But not this way."

His eyes opened and looked into hers. "You think I'm not capable of love?" he asked, with a note of despair in his voice.

Beth held herself back from putting her arms around him again. He sounded as if he was worried about the issue himself.

"I think you're capable of great love," she answered quietly. "But you have to take a chance with your feelings first. And somehow I know that will be very difficult for you."

He didn't answer, merely picked up the hand that had touched his face and kissed it. Then, without a word, he walked to the door and left.

Beth went back into the living room and made the drink she'd refused earlier. She heard Bram's car start, and she sat in the stillness long after the sound of the motor had faded into silence.

Bram was the only man she had ever wanted, and she had let him go. He was the only lover she had ever desired; in fact, she had never had another. But Bram didn't know that. He didn't know that she had turned away, disappointed and disillusioned, from every other man who had tried to make love to her.

Beth put down her drink. She folded her hands in her lap and considered her situation.

She was in love with Bram, and had been since she'd seen him standing on her lawn, talking to her sister on that summer night so long ago. It seemed such a ridiculous notion to her trained mind, that she could have fallen in love in the space of a few hours and then carried that torch, still burning brightly, through the succeeding years. Ever since she'd returned to Suffield she'd been trying to talk herself out of it, but tonight she conceded defeat. She had known better when she was in high school; there had been no doubt that Fourth of July that she was in love with Bram, or she never would have let things get as far as they had. She'd been full of romantic ideas in those days, waiting for a dashing stranger to appear and sweep her off her feet. But that was exactly what had happened, and she'd accepted it at the time. It was a rude awakening to realize that her instincts had been better when she was a teenager than they were now.

Now she was full of fears and anxieties that held her back from reaching for the only thing in life she had ever truly wanted.

Beth stood and walked to the window, looking out across the lawn, half wishing that she could turn back into the girl she had been once. Then, in her innocence, she had responded instantly to Bram's presence, ignited by the flame of his ardor, certain that it must be the same for him as it was for her. How wonderful to be so sure in a matter of an evening that you had found the man who would determine the rest of your life.

Beth let the curtain fall and turned back into the room.

But what if the man didn't feel the same?

4

Beth looked up as Mindy staggered through the door, her face hidden behind a gigantic box of manila file folders. She lurched into the room and dropped the box, collapsing in the nearest folding chair.

"I got you supplies to outfit three offices," she announced to Beth, wiping her brow with the back of her hand. "You have enough files to last a year."

"I have more files than clients," Beth answered. "I wish I had something to put in the folders."

"You will, you will," Mindy reassured her. "I'm doing my best to get the word around."

Beth eyed her narrowly. "What does that mean?"

Mindy shifted her weight nervously. "Don't be so

suspicious. I just gave a few people your card, that's all."

"And where did you get my card?"

"There was a box of them sitting on the desk after you got them from the printer," Mindy replied. "I took some of them."

Beth put her hands on her hips. "Mindy," she said in a stern tone, "if you've been handing them out on street corners . . ."

Mindy feigned outrage. "Don't be ridiculous. My husband is a lawyer; I know better than that. But I have slipped them to a few friends."

Beth was about to pursue this subject further when the phone rang. Beth stepped over the pile of books on the floor and picked up the receiver.

"This is Bram," a masculine voice said without preliminary. "You never said whether you would take over the legal work for Curtis Broadleaf."

Startled, Beth didn't answer.

"You still there?" he asked crisply. "I can't wait all day."

"I . . . well, I guess so," Beth answered, flustered. The stacks of empty files did not bolster her original conviction to turn him down. "Can I let you know tomorrow? I'd like to think about it."

"Think fast," Bram barked. "I have some contracts that need attention, pronto." The line went dead.

Beth slammed the receiver into its cradle. "I am going to kill that man," she said grimly.

"Who?" Mindy asked innocently. When Beth looked at her, Mindy's eyes shifted away.

"Take a wild guess," Beth said dryly. "You gave Bram my office number, didn't you?"

"Why not?" Mindy defended herself. "You need

the business, and your number will be published in a couple of days. You're acting like I gave him the secret code to the red phone at the White House."

"All right, all right," Beth muttered. She picked up a volume of the Connecticut Penal Code and put it down again. The carpenter was coming to install bookshelves in what had formerly been a downstairs bedroom, and until he did there was no way to alleviate much of the chaos.

"Have you seen Bram since the day after Marion's reception?" Mindy asked quietly.

"No."

Mindy bit the edge of her thumb. "You really should represent him, you know," she advised. "It's not as though you're turning away clients at the door."

"You noticed," Beth smiled humorlessly.

"Things will pick up," Mindy said. "Your father was well known; your name will mean something."

"My father is dead, and his friends were raised in a generation that took a Victorian view of women. I don't think any of them are going to beat down my door."

"All the more reason to do the work for Bram," Mindy said slyly. "If you make a success of it, everyone will be impressed."

"If I botch it, everyone will pat me on the head and tell me to leave the important issues to the men."

"You're not going to botch it."

"How do you know? I saw the background material on Bram's company, and some of the deals they make with the growers and the processors are pretty complex."

"So read up on it. You can read, can't you? It sounds to me like you're trying to talk yourself out of it, and you can't afford to do that. Are you afraid of seeing Bram?"

"Of course not," Beth replied, turning her head.

"Hmm," Mindy said. "Since the age of seven you could never look at me directly when you were telling a lie."

"Okay, so the thought of working with him makes me uncomfortable. Is that so hard to understand?"

Mindy stood abruptly. "I can understand it, but my advice to you is to swallow your misgivings and get out the legal pads. Bram is handing you a golden opportunity on a silver platter and you'd better grab it."

"I guess you're right," Beth conceded wearily.

"Well, I'm off to pick up Thing One and Thing Two from my mother's," Mindy said, shouldering her purse. She was referring to her little girls, so called after a children's book that featured characters of the same name. "If anything arrives, like the arc lamp, the desk blotter, or a phalanx of new clients, give me a call."

Beth nodded. "Thanks a lot, Mindy, you've been a big help. I didn't know what to order from those office supply places. You worked wonders."

"I've outfitted a new office every time Hal's changed jobs," Mindy said dryly. "I could make a career out of it."

The phone rang again, and Mindy waved good-bye as Beth answered it.

"It's probably the attorney general," she whispered, and made a face. Beth grinned at her disappearing back.

But it was only the business machine company, asking when the electric typewriter could be delivered. As Beth glanced at the yellow bill of sale, totaling up the amount due, she resolved to take Bram on as a client and charge him a whopping retainer.

At least then she would be able to pay for the typewriter.

Two days later Beth pushed through the glass double doors of the Semple Building in downtown Hartford, glancing up at the business roster framed on the wall in the entrance hall. Curtis Broadleaf was on the third floor, sharing it with another firm. Old Joshua Curtis must have been doing all right before Bram's return, Beth reflected wryly; his company was occupying some of Hartford's prime real estate. She playfully adjusted the amount she would request upward, and then giggled, shaking her head. She knew she would be fair and ask only what was reasonable under the circumstances, but it amused her to imagine Bram's stunned reaction when she threw out a highly inflated figure. He'd pay it anyway, she admitted to herself. Damn him, he could afford to, and they both knew it.

She rode the elevator up to the third floor and stepped from it into an atmosphere of hushed luxury. Deep eggshell carpeting silenced her footsteps as she walked to the reception desk, and the walls, covered with cream grasscloth and edged with mahogany wainscoting, held photographs and certificates attesting to Joshua's standing in the community. An immaculately dressed and coiffed secretary looked up at Beth's approach.

"I'm Attorney Forsyth," Beth said to the woman. "I called yesterday and made an appointment to see Mr. Curtis at three today."

"Mr. Curtis is ill at home," the woman said smoothly. "There must be some mistake. I can arrange for you to see Miss Wyler, Mr. Curtis's administrative assistant, but I'm afraid . . ."

"Mr. *Abraham* Curtis," Beth interrupted her. "I confirmed the time with him myself." During a very brief conversation, Beth added silently. Bram had hung up as if the phone were on fire in his hand.

The secretary, who looked about thirty and had doubtless intimidated many who'd tried to breach the Curtis defenses with her cool, blond beauty and sophisticated air, arched a thin eyebrow. "I wasn't aware Mr. Abraham was seeing anyone today."

Mr. Abraham, Beth thought in amazement. Had she suddenly entered a time warp and emerged on an antebellum plantation? She glanced at the nameplate on the desk and tried again.

"Miss Langley, I assure you that I'm not some panhandler who has decided to pass herself off as a lawyer. If you will just be kind enough to ring Mr. Curtis, I'm certain he'll clear this up for you."

"That won't be necessary, Gloria," Bram announced as he emerged from the elevator that had brought Beth. "I'll take Miss Forsyth to my office." He smiled at Gloria, who retreated visibly, like a guard dog responding to an order to heel.

Beth turned and met his eyes. He glanced at her neutrally and gestured for her to come with him.

Beth looked back at Gloria and caught an instant of naked hostility in the secretary's expression before she donned a carefully smooth mask of efficiency and went back to her typing. Beth's eyes flashed to Bram, but if he had caught the exchange between the two women he gave no sign.

Beth followed him to a door at the end of the hall. It

led to an office paneled in oak and furnished with exquisite antique pieces. It was obviously Bram's father's, and Beth waited uncomfortably while Bram went to a filing cabinet and extracted a leather binder from a drawer.

"Have a seat," he said casually, and Beth sat stiffly in a chair that faced the large table desk. It was set in a niche in front of a bay window overlooking the city. Bram walked to the swivel chair behind the desk and dropped into it, crossing one leg over the other knee. He tossed the binder onto the desk between them, as if it were a bone of contention.

"There you go," he said, a subtle challenge in his tone. "Have a ball."

Beth picked it up and put it in her briefcase. "I'll look these over tonight and call you in the morning. Is there anything I should know before I get started on them?"

Bram examined her with eyes the color of a dark French brandy. He was wearing a navy crew-neck sweater with jeans and tennis shoes, and looked more like a spectator at a lacrosse match than the top executive in a tobacco empire.

"The first contract is rather complicated," he said, opening an envelope on his desk. "I have my copy here. Do you want to go over it?"

Beth nodded, and they spent about an hour comparing ideas on the work Beth had to do. She was impressed with Bram's grasp of the business; she knew he'd been back only a short time and yet he was familiar with all aspects of the operation. He must have been doing his homework, Beth thought. It was a pity he'd spent all those years sailing around the world when he might have been taking his rightful place beside his father. But Bram's choices were his own to make, and she had nothing to say about them.

She realized that he was staring at her. "What?" she said, confused.

"I said it's almost four-thirty, and asked if you'd like to get a drink. I'm through for the day, and you should be, too."

Beth picked up her purse, not answering.

"Just a drink, Beth," he said quietly. "That's all."

Beth met his eyes. His were intent, measuring.

"Okay," she said, standing up.

His lips twisted as he moved to walk out beside her. "Very gracious of you," he commented dryly.

Gloria looked up from her Dictaphone as they passed, and her glance took in the two of them heading for the door. "Going home?" she asked, in a mild tone that belied her tense posture.

"Yes," Bram replied shortly. "Take any messages for me and leave them on my desk. I'll see you in the morning, Gloria."

Beth felt Gloria's eyes burning into her back as they stepped onto the elevator. She wasn't fooled by Gloria's pleasant tone. The woman took a proprietary interest in her boss that had nothing to do with her secretarial duties.

"There's a place just across the street," Bram said as they descended. "It's quiet and caters to the rush-hour crowd."

"Fine," Beth answered, looking away from him.

Bram sighed and ran a big hand through his thick hair. "Bethany, if you're going to speak in monosyllables, we might as well call this off right now. I asked you to come with me because I wanted to talk to *you*, not myself."

Beth examined him with narrowed eyes. "Why?"

He blinked. "Why?" he repeated.

"Yes. Why did you want to talk to me?"

He threw his hands out in exasperation. "Because I like you," he said, shrugging slightly.

Beth turned her head so he couldn't see her silent struggle against the flood of emotion his words had released. He had an unerring knack for saying just the thing to disarm her.

The elevator reached the ground floor and the doors slid open. Bram put his hand on Beth's shoulder to guide her through the departing crowd and sent a river of sensation down her arm. She stiffened at his touch; he felt it and removed his hand.

"Relax," he said in her ear as he pushed the door open in front of them. Beth pressed her lips together. If only she could.

They stepped out into a cool fall evening, freshened by a sunset breeze. Beth turned her face up to catch it, inhaling deeply.

Bram pointed over her shoulder at the facade of a lounge on the other side of the road. "Come on," he said, when the light changed. They jogged across the street together, weaving through the idling cars waiting for the light. When they entered the dim restaurant the hostess greeted Bram by name and led them to a booth in an alcove at the back.

"What would you like?" he asked, as the waiter hovered in the background.

Beth looked blank.

"Still a heavy drinker, I see," Bram said, smiling,

and motioned to the hostess. He ordered a Scotch for himself and something with a foreign-sounding name for Beth.

"What's that?" she asked suspiciously.

"A liqueur, very mild. I think you'll like it." He grinned, his eyes dancing, tilting his head to one side. "Don't you trust me?" he asked.

"Not for a second," Beth replied grimly, and he laughed.

"Do you mind if I ask you a question?" he said suddenly, still smiling.

"Go ahead. I don't promise I'll answer it."

He nodded. "Fair enough. Why did you decide to take me on as a client? I had the distinct impression you had almost made up your mind to turn me down."

"I need the money," Beth said.

He was silent a moment, and then snorted, taking a handful of peanuts from the wooden bowl on the table. "I guess that's telling me. I was flattering myself that it had something to do with your inability to resist my fatal charm."

Beth clasped her fingers together on the tabletop. "Your charm is fatal enough, you don't need me to tell you that," she said softly.

She heard his indrawn breath. "Bethany . . ." he began.

Beth held up her hand. "No. Let me finish. You hurt me, Bram. You hurt me so much that I resolved to stay away from you and never give you the chance to do it again."

He listened, his eyes fixed on her face.

"But practical considerations outweighed the emotional ones. Your account will be lucrative, and if I handle it well it'll give me some needed publicity around town. I could use both the cash and the goodwill."

Bram nodded slowly. "I see. Oh, for the good old days when a woman told a man only what he wanted to hear."

"I think they went out with the hoop skirt," Beth said.

"I find myself longing for their return when I'm in your company," Bram said dryly.

Their drinks arrived, and Bram took a sip of his before he asked, "Why do you need money? I thought your father left everything to you and your sister."

"He left us the house, but everything else is tied up in trust until each of us reaches thirty. Marion will get her share next year, but I have to wait three more years. Right now I'm living in a mansion that I can barely afford to run."

Bram twirled the ice cubes in his glass. "Bethany, if you need a loan—"

"No, thank you," Beth said firmly, cutting him off. "I'll earn my own way."

"I believe you will," he replied quietly. "But the offer stands, if you ever want to take me up on it."

Beth picked up her drink and tasted it. The liquid, a dark rose-pink, was faintly sweet and flavored by the slice of lemon floating at the bottom of the glass. "It's good," she said.

Bram inclined his head. "I'm glad you approve."

"You must be accustomed to selecting beverages for ladies," she observed.

"I'm accustomed to ordering for women," Bram answered shortly. "I don't know how many of them I would call ladies."

"How would you categorize Gloria?" Beth asked, and then could have bitten off her tongue. Why on earth did she say that?

Bram took another swallow of his drink and thought a moment before he answered. "I'm surprised my attorney would be interested in my opinion on that subject."

"I shouldn't have brought it up; it's none of my business," Beth said quickly.

"What makes you think there's anything between Gloria and me?" Bram inquired.

"She practically threw herself in my path trying to keep me away from you this afternoon, and when she saw us leaving together she gave me the death ray," Beth stated flatly. "I got the impression she thinks of you as her territory."

"And she views you as a potential poacher?" Bram asked.

"She seems to. I hope she doesn't take that attitude with every woman who comes to see you."

"Gloria takes her job very seriously," Bram said evenly.

"How nice for you," Beth responded tightly.

Bram gazed at her across the expanse of the polished table. "If I didn't know better, I'd say you were jealous," he murmured softly.

Beth looked at him, and then away. "I am," she said. "I'm jealous of any woman you ever looked at, and I probably always will be."

Bram's lips parted, and his fingers tightened around the glass he was holding. "Damn it, Beth. How the hell do you expect me to keep my distance when you say something like that to me?"

"I expect you to keep your distance because we want different things from each other."

Bram's dark eyes raked her, and she felt a finger of fire tracing her body. "You know what I want," he said huskily.

"Yes," she whispered.

"What do you want?" he asked in the same lazy, intimate tone.

Beth reached across the table and placed her palm over his heart. "I want what's in here," she said quietly. "I want what you withhold from everybody. And until you're willing to give it, I'm your lawyer, you're my client, and that's it."

Bram exhaled slowly as she withdrew her hand, and then drained the rest of the liquor in his glass. "Lady, you drive a hard bargain," he said darkly.

A waiter arrived and asked if they wanted a second round. Bram ordered another for himself after Beth shook her head to decline.

"What happens if I don't obey the ground rules?" Bram asked as soon as the man went back to the bar.

"Don't you intend to?" Beth responded.

"I make no promises," he said levelly, his eyes straying to her mouth.

"Then I'll have to be on my guard, won't I?" Beth said.

"You're always on your guard," Bram observed sarcastically.

He sounded so genuinely annoyed that she had to smile.

"What's funny?" Bram asked.

"You don't like opposition, do you?" Beth asked.

"Does anyone?"

"I have a feeling that other people have a little more experience in dealing with it than you do. When somebody puts a roadblock in your path, you either crash through it or decide it isn't worth the effort and walk away. You don't go in much for negotiation."

"Which will it be with you?" he asked, his gaze penetrating.

"I don't know. It appears that with your father you just walked away."

Bram nodded as the waiter deposited another scotch in front of him, and then he downed half of it. "There's no other way to deal with Joshua. He's too stubborn and opinionated for subtler tactics," Bram said.

"Sounds like somebody else I know," Beth observed innocently.

Bram ignored that. "The old man actually did me a favor," he went on, as if she hadn't spoken. "I got a chance to get out and see the world, and acquired a finer education than he could have bought for me at an Ivy League school. I've often thought that I should thank him."

"Did you ever discuss it?" Beth persisted. "Did you ever talk to him about why you left?"

Bram's expression hardened. "We don't talk about anything but the business. He prefers to leave the rest of it in the past, and frankly, so do I."

"But don't you see that you'll never be comfortable with each other until you settle your old differences? My father is dead, Bram, and believe me, I wish every day that I had tried to make peace with him. We just glossed over those old wounds and let them fester."

"You mean like the wound I inflicted when I seduced you in his den?" Bram asked.

"You didn't seduce me," Beth answered in a low tone.

"I would have," Bram countered. "If your father hadn't arrived when he did you would have lost your virginity to me that night." He smiled sadly. "Instead I left you to a stranger's hands."

No, you didn't, Beth thought.

"I hope the experience was good for you," Bram added.

Beth said nothing.

"Many times I've wished that it had been me," Bram concluded. "That is just one of a long line of my regrets, but I think it sits at the top of the list."

Beth realized that he had had two stiff drinks on what was probably an empty stomach. He was doubtless a little drunk; he didn't open up easily, and he was revealing a little too much for total sobriety.

"I think I'd better be going," she said nervously. "It's getting late."

He saluted her with a glass that contained only ice cubes. "Forgive me. I'm bringing up a sensitive subject. I don't mean to drive you out the door."

"You're not. I have to get home. Mindy's husband is bringing over a potential client tonight, somebody in real estate who needs a lawyer to do closings and title searches, that sort of thing."

"Who?" Bram asked suspiciously.

"Jason Raines. He and his brother own Raines Realty."

Bram nodded, grimacing. "I know him. He's a stiff."

Beth sighed, exasperated. "I don't care about his personality, Bram."

Bram's brow furrowed. "I think I broke his nose in a fight once."

Beth groaned. "Wonderful. I'll remember not to mention your name."

Bram snapped his fingers. "It wasn't Jason, it was his brother Ronald. It doesn't matter, they're both blockheads."

"Nevertheless, I assume their money is green," Beth said, standing up. "I'll go over those papers tonight and call you in the morning."

Bram rose also. "I'll walk you to your car."

"That isn't necessary."

Bram deposited several bills on the table and took her arm. "Yes, it is. A woman was mugged not two blocks from here only last week."

"Bram, this is the Hartford business district, and it isn't even dark yet."

"Are you going to argue with me about this now?" he asked, steering her through the door.

"Okay, okay. The car is just around the corner."

When they reached the parking lot Beth paused beside her little green sports car and took her keys from her purse.

"Thanks for escorting me to the door," she said formally.

"Thanks for taking my case," Bram replied, extending his hand.

When Beth reached out to shake it he held her fingers to his lips. Her eyes closed at the warm touch of his mouth, the bristling softness of his mustache. Then she straightened and pulled her hand away.

"No fair," she said in a soft, warning tone.

"A minor infraction," Bram pleaded.

"I expect you to treat me as you would any other lawyer who worked for you. Would you have kissed Don Matheson's hand?"

Bram started to laugh. "Point taken," he conceded. He stood back and folded his arms as she got into the car and started the engine. When she rolled down the window he leaned on the sill and looked in at her.

"What was the name of that little dog you used to have?" he asked.

Beth blinked, confused. "What?"

"That little dog, you told me about him the night of your father's party. He had a name like a prison, San Quentin or Leavenworth, something like that."

"Alcatraz," Beth supplied, wondering what had uprooted that memory.

"Right. Alcatraz. God, your face when you talked about him, so sad and so sweet. I wanted to kiss you until you couldn't breathe."

Hit the road, Bethany, she instructed herself. Don't stick around for any more of this, or all your resolutions are going to flow down the drain.

"Bram," she said firmly, "I really have to go. I'll talk to you tomorrow." She waited pointedly until he moved away from the window, and then rolled it up smartly. With a cheerful wave she drove away, feigning a brightness she didn't feel.

This was going to be awfully difficult. Just being with him was an endurance test. How could she hope to work with him on a business level and keep all of her turbulent feelings in check?

One day at a time, she thought as she pulled out onto the highway that would take her back to Suffield. She would just have to deal with it one day at a time.

5

~oooooooooo~

Jason Raines *was* a stiff, or maybe it was just the contrast with the memory of Bram's imposing presence that afternoon. Beth was happy to leave him with Hal to discuss some political issue in which she had no interest. She wandered into the kitchen, where Mindy was trying to persuade Tracy to drink a glass of milk.

"How did it go?" Mindy asked, looking up from her daughter.

"Okay, I guess. He has a reasonable amount of work for me. The lawyer who used to handle his account moved to Florida. So it looks like I'm the choice to take over for him."

Mindy studied her. "You could seem a bit happier about it."

Beth shrugged. "I am happy about it. Just preoccupied."

"With Bram?"

"What do you have, Melinda Sue? Radar?"

Mindy shook her head. "Twenty years experience dealing with you. You told him you'd represent him, didn't you?"

"Yes. I'm going to be up all night reading the mound of papers he gave me."

"But that isn't what has you worried."

"Come on, Mindy, you know it isn't. How am I going to work for him and not get involved with him?"

"Search me. I'm glad it's not my problem."

"You're a great comfort, Mindy."

"Hey. I don't know what to tell you. I don't know how to handle him, I don't even think it's *possible* to handle him. Just do your job and hope for the best."

"What is the best? I tell myself I shouldn't get involved with him, but when I'm with him I feel alive, and when I'm not with him I miss him so much."

"Sounds like love to me," Mindy said.

"It's totally one-sided."

"I wouldn't agree with that. He's definitely interested."

"He's interested in getting me into bed. That's about it."

"Yeah, well, he's famous in that department," Mindy commented, tilting the glass she held so that another stream of milk ran down her daughter's throat. Tracy swallowed obediently.

Beth was instantly alert. "What have you heard?"

Mindy shrugged. "That that bombshell of a secretary who works for Curtis is apparently indulging in some extracurricular activity with the boss's son."

"Tell me something I don't know," Beth responded gloomily.

"You've met her?" Mindy asked.

"Uh-huh. This afternoon at Bram's office. If looks could kill, you'd be ordering flowers for my funeral right now."

"Maybe that's a good sign. She must be worried. Also, I seem to remember something about a doctor at Johnson Memorial. She treated him for a sprained ankle after a softball game and wound up going out with him."

"That sounds like Bram," Beth said, sighing. "He doesn't believe in wasting any opportunities."

Mindy wiped Tracy's chin thoughtfully. "And wasn't Claire Breen telling me that she saw Bram with some brunette who worked at one of the radio stations downtown? Yes, she said they were at a restaurant and he introduced her as the assistant station manager, something like that."

Beth groaned with real feeling. "Enough already. I'm sorry I asked. I wonder how he has the energy to drag himself to work every day."

Hal entered the kitchen, glancing at his watch. "Honey, shouldn't we be going? We have to pick Lisa up at your mother's in half an hour."

Lisa was Mindy's younger daughter, alternately known as Thing Two.

Mindy stood and began inserting Tracy's arms into the sleeves of her sweater. Jason came up behind Hal and said to Beth, "Do you think I could have another cup of that coffee for the road?"

"Sure," Beth replied, going to get it. She hoped Jason wasn't planning to stay behind and turn the evening into an opportunity to get to know her better.

He was. He lingered after she had shown Mindy and family to the door, asking her about law school and her plans for her practice. Beth tried to be polite, but after about twenty minutes of pleasant but distant conversation, Jason took the hint and went home. Beth feared that he had not given up, however, and sensed that he would try again in the future.

After Jason left Beth went into the downstairs powder room and splashed cold water on her face, trying to revive herself for the task of poring over Bram's file. She glanced in the mirror as she turned to go and wondered if she was looking at a fool. Jason was attractive, intelligent, and well-to-do, with what her father would have referred to as "good prospects." He was a tall, slender blond with green eyes and a shy smile. Why didn't she like him? She knew the answer. He wasn't Bram. She was crazy about a bearded rogue who would probably hang around just long enough for his father to get well and then go off to sea again. There was no future in that, but she couldn't seem to change her feelings.

She folded the towel neatly on the rack and pulled the door shut behind her. She wasn't going to worry about that now. She had work to do.

During the next three weeks Beth met with Bram frequently to assist him with his legal problems.

He asked her to dinner three times. She refused.

He asked her to go for a drink with him five times. She refused.

He asked her to a hockey game, an anniversary

party, and the grand opening of a new theater. She refused.

Beth was not enjoying herself. The constant strain of saying no when she really wanted to say yes was fraying her nerves. But she stuck to her guns and kept their contact on a purely professional level.

At first Bram treated her stand with tolerant indulgence. But as time passed and he saw that she had no intention of giving in, his attitude became increasingly hostile. Things deteriorated to the point where they were conducting their business in an atmosphere fraught with tension, speaking to each other with frigid politeness and walking on eggshells lest either of them disturb the delicate balance. Bram's withdrawn silences, his measured glances cut Beth to the quick, and the undertone of mild sarcasm she well remembered from earlier conversations had resurfaced with a vengeance. She was at her wits' end. She didn't know what to do. If she began to see him socially she was headed for trouble, but there was a limit to how much more of his icy manner she could endure.

In late September the Chamber of Commerce was holding a fund-raiser for the United Way, and Jason Raines invited Beth to attend with him. At first she hesitated; such affairs always seemed phony to her, an excuse for local politicians and business people to get together and toot their own horns. But Jason finally convinced her to go along. She had to admit that she could use the exposure, and realized that she'd better get used to such socializing if she expected to build up a practice.

The night before the party she was trying on various dresses, unable to decide what to wear, while Marion sat on the edge of her bed and offered a running commentary on each outfit. Marion's husband was away for the weekend, and she had driven up from New York that afternoon to visit her sister.

"That's too short," Marion announced as Beth pirouetted in front of the mirror. "It's always been too short. I don't know why you bought it in the first place."

"I bought it because it was on sale," Beth replied, examining the sweep of the dress against her ankles.

"That isn't going to make it any longer," Marion replied.

Beth shot her a look and reached for the zipper at the back of her neck. "All right," she said. "That narrows it down to a choice between the aqua chiffon and the red silk."

"Don't you have anything else?"

"No, Marion, I don't. My wardrobe of formal wear is severely limited. We didn't go in much for gowns at the law firm in Boston where I worked."

"Then buy something."

Beth slipped out of the dress she was wearing and put it back on the hanger. It was easy for Marion to say; her husband's family minted money in their cellar out on Long Island. If Beth splurged on an expensive dress, she would be skimping on ribbons for her typewriter.

"It'll have to be the chiffon," she said, taking it out of her closet.

"What about the red one?" Marion asked, crossing her legs.

"It makes me look like a chorus girl. That's not exactly the impression I'm trying to create." Beth donned the aqua dress and let Marion fasten it. She stepped back to the mirror and both women were silent as they examined the effect.

"I think it's out of style," Marion finally said.

Beth slumped in disappointment. "What am I going to do? I already told Jason I would go with him."

"Does Mindy have anything?" Marion asked.

Beth stared at her sister. "You know Mindy's taste. Everything she owns looks great on her and makes me look like an embroidered lampshade."

Marion stood up suddenly. "Wait a minute. I left some of my things in the closet in my room when I moved out. They're still there. Remember that off-white strapless number I got for last New Year's Eve? The fabric's light—I think you could get away with it. I'll be right back."

Marion went down the hall to her old bedroom and Beth replaced the aqua dress in the closet. She was standing barefoot in her slip when Marion returned with the dress.

Beth had forgotten how pretty it was. She and Marion had similar coloring and were almost the same height and weight, so it fit. The draped bodice tapered to a fitted waist and the shirred skirt featured a side slit that bared a portion of one graceful leg. Beth stepped into her shoes and studied her reflection in the mirror.

"There you go," Marion said triumphantly. "It looks as if it were made for you. Put your hair up, and with a necklace and earrings it'll be perfect. I have a lace shawl that will go great with it, too."

Beth hugged her sister. "Marion, you're a lifesaver." She was turning to glance at the rear view when Marion said, "Is Bram going to this shindig?"

"Don't be ridiculous," Beth replied. "Bram wouldn't be caught dead at one of these things."

Marion raised her brows. "I wouldn't be too sure. Joshua is certain to get a courtesy invitation, and Hal told me that Bram's been taking his place at a lot of functions recently. If I were you, I'd be prepared to see him."

"It never occurred to me that he might go," Beth said thoughtfully.

Marion shrugged. "Ordinarily I would agree with you, but he's been trying to cooperate with Joshua lately. If his father wants him to go, he'll be there."

Beth absorbed that in silence.

"That obviously bothers you," Marion said.

Beth sighed.

"I don't understand," Marion went on. "I thought you were working with him. Aren't you getting along?"

Beth removed Marion's gown and folded it over her arm. "That's one way of putting it."

Marion pursed her lips. "Okay, Bethany, I may not have a cum laude law degree but even I can see that something is up with you. What's going on?"

"I should never have agreed to represent Curtis Broadleaf."

"Why? Is it too much for you?"

"No, no. I did a lot of reading on corporate contracts to familiarize myself with the sort of work I would have to do, but once I got into the swing of it I was okay. I've been handling it pretty well."

"Then it *is* Bram."

"Yes."

Marion took the dress away from Beth and put it

back in its protective plastic bag. "Well, I can't say I'm surprised. You two have always been a volatile combination."

"He's forever pushing for a personal relationship, and I'm afraid to get involved with him. You know what he's like."

"I know what he's like," Marion confirmed grimly.

"And the more I resist, the more hostile and defensive he becomes. He's retreated behind this wall of excessive politeness; every word he says sets my teeth on edge. We're circling each other like a pair of . . . of . . ."

"Tigers about to mate?" Marion suggested.

"I wish you wouldn't be quite so graphic," Beth said faintly.

"It's the image that comes to mind," Marion said crisply. "I've never seen such chemistry. I've often thought that you two were destined for something."

"Yes. Disaster."

Marion shook her head. "That's not what I'd call it." She eyed her sister sympathetically. "He takes your breath away, doesn't he?"

Beth swallowed, and then nodded.

"Well, then, I'd say you're lucky. Most people never feel that way about anybody." She reached out and patted Beth's arm. "You'll cope with it."

"I'm not so sure."

"I am," Marion said in a definite tone. "You're the only woman I know who could take that guy on and hold her own." She headed for the door. "I'll see if I can dig up that shawl."

"Thanks," Beth called after her, bemused by the tone of admiration in her sister's voice. Marion was not one for tossing bouquets; she really seemed to think Beth was equal to the task of handling Bram Curtis.

Sis, I hope you're right, Beth thought. She glanced at the pile of garments decorating her bed and set about putting them away.

The next night was cool and clear, and Beth was ready when Jason came to get her in his dark blue Volvo. He looked neat and attractive in his evening clothes, and complimented Beth lavishly on her appearance. The party was being held in one of the ballrooms of the Sonesta Hotel in downtown Hartford, and the affair was already under way as they entered.

The first person Beth saw was Bram. He was dressed in a black tuxedo with a gray cummerbund and gray bow tie, accented by a silk shirt that flashed polished buttons when he moved. On his arm was a tall, dazzling redhead in a low-cut green dress. He turned as Beth walked through the door with Jason, and his eyes met hers. He stared at her for several seconds, and then bent to make a comment to the woman with him. She laughed, and Beth looked away.

"You okay?" Jason asked.

"Of course," Beth said quickly. "Where's our table?"

Jason led the way to their seats, and then went to the bar to get them both a drink. Beth found herself talking to one of her tablemates, the wife of a prominent surgeon who was an officer in the local United Way chapter. The conversation diverted Beth until the woman said, "Oh, there's Dr. Reynolds. Who's that dark man with her?"

She was talking about Bram's date. "She's a doctor?" Beth asked, her heart sinking.

"Yes," her companion said. "Couldn't you just kill yourself? She's on staff at Johnson Memorial with my husband. Can you imagine looking like that and having brains, too? No wonder she can snare such a handsome date."

The sprained-ankle specialist, Beth thought glumly. This was the woman Mindy had mentioned. Beth watched as Dr. Reynolds whispered something in Bram's ear, and his dazzling grin flashed from across the room. Beth sighed. It was beginning to look like a long night.

Jason returned, and once dinner was served Beth began to feel better. Bram and his friend were seated on the far side of the dance floor, and they were obscured by several potted palms, so Beth was spared the sight of their mealtime conviviality. But during the interlude before dessert the band started to play and Jason asked her to dance. She didn't see how she could gracefully refuse, so she walked with him onto the floor. Jason was a correct if spiritless dancer, and Beth was able to follow him effortlessly until the conclusion of the set. As they applauded with the rest of the group, she realized that Jason was standing next to Bram.

Beth tugged on his arm to capture his attention, but it was too late. Jason had noticed the man at his side.

"Here's one of your clients, Bethie," he announced in a delighted tone that made Beth want to hit him with a rock. "It's Curtis, isn't it?" Jason said to Bram. "I seem to remember selling a summerhouse to your father."

Bram turned, favoring Jason with a cool, dark glance. "Yes, my father is fond of buying things. You may also recall that when we were all in high school I put your brother in the hospital."

Beth closed her eyes as the men shook hands.

Jason chuckled. "Yeah, Ronnie always was a hothead. Well, it looks like I'm here with your lawyer, Curtis."

Bram looked at Beth. "So it appears," he said evenly. Only Beth detected the edge in his tone. "Hello, counselor."

Beth nodded, wishing that she was home watching reruns on television.

"May I introduce Althea Reynolds?" Bram was saying. He took the redhead's hand and brought her forward. "Thea, this is my lawyer, Bethany Forsyth. Beth, my doctor, Althea Reynolds."

The two women eyed each other as Jason beamed.

"How do you do?" Beth murmured.

Dr. Reynolds smiled, displaying perfect teeth.

"You're doing all right, Curtis," Jason chuckled. "My doctor is sixty-five years old, with an arthritic hip."

"I'm sure *Bethie* will help you get in touch with the changing times," Bram said mildly. Beth didn't miss the slight emphasis on the nickname, which he knew she didn't like.

Mercifully, the music began again, and Beth seized Jason, practically dragging him across the floor.

"Good seeing you, Bram," she babbled, steering Jason away. "Nice to meet you, Dr. Reynolds." She had hustled Jason to the opposite end of the floor before he had a chance to object.

"You seemed anxious to get away from those two," Jason observed in what was surely the understatement of the year. "Don't you like Curtis?"

"Don't be silly," Beth replied. "Isn't the music lovely?"

"Sure," Jason answered, looking down at her with a bewildered expression. "This is the same band they had at the Lions Club Christmas party last year."

"Isn't that interesting?" Beth said brightly. "I guess you have to attend quite a few of these functions."

She was able to engage Jason in conversation until he suggested that they return to their table and have dessert. They were about to do so when Bram materialized from nowhere and tapped Jason on the shoulder.

"I wonder if I might borrow your date for this dance," Bram said shortly.

Jason stepped back and released Beth. "See you back at the table, Bethie," he said cheerfully.

Bram moved in smoothly and took Beth in his arms. "Enjoying yourself, Bethie?" he asked mildly.

"I'm having a wonderful time," she answered, trying not to react to the smell of Bram's shaving soap, the feel of his body next to hers. This was the closest she'd been to him in weeks, and her senses were responding accordingly.

"Oh, I can see that you are," Bram said. "Raines looks like stimulating company."

"He's very nice," Beth said stiffly.

"Really?" Bram inquired, arching one dark brow. "What do you talk about with him? Interest rates? Closing fees? The availability of mortgage money?" He steered her past the clustered tables and into an alcove near the hall.

"Jason is accomplished and well read," Beth said. "You'd be surprised at what we have in common."

"I'd be surprised, all right," Bram muttered darkly. He stopped dancing and pulled Beth after him out of the ballroom and past the hatcheck girl, who looked up in amazement. Beth tried to wrench free as Bram shoved her into the dim, empty lobby.

"Let me go!" she demanded. "What do you think you're doing?"

"I'm getting you away from that bunch of solid citizens in there," he whispered.

"You can't make me stay here," Beth fumed. "I'll cause a scene."

He smiled. "Go ahead. Do you think I care? I'd scandalized half of the valley several times by my eighteenth birthday; it'll be nothing new for me."

Beth closed her mouth. He was right. She was the one with something to lose.

Bram advanced on her as he saw her relent. He took her chin in his hand and gazed down into her eyes.

"Do you let him kiss you?" he asked softly. "Do you let him make love to you?"

Beth couldn't answer, riveted by his dark gaze.

"You won't let me touch you," he whispered. "You run all over town with that . . . that . . . dullard, and I can't come near you." He seized her wrists and pulled them up next to her face, pinning her. "Why, mouse? Why?"

Beth's lips parted, but no sound escaped them.

"Have you forgotten what it was like with me?" he rasped. "Let me remind you." He took a step forward and his lips crushed hers.

Beth tried to resist, but her body refused to obey the

commands of her mind. Her mouth opened under his as he enfolded her in an embrace that left her limp, clinging to him.

Bram bent his head, and his lips trailed over her exposed shoulder. "Your skin is like silk," he muttered. "The feel of it, the scent of it has been in my blood for ten years."

Beth sank her fingers into his hair, holding his head against her. She felt so weak that without his support she would have fallen.

Bram's hands moved up from her waist, over her back. He braced her against him with one arm and slipped the fingers of his other hand inside the top of her dress. Beth gasped as he caressed her breast, his thumb probing her swollen nipple.

"Such response," he murmured, his lips against her neck. "You turn to me like a flower seeking the sun."

Beth swayed in his arms as the room spun around her.

"Don't fight it," Bram urged, his mouth creating a stream of heat all along her throat. "Give in. Give in to what you feel for me."

"I can't," Beth moaned, and at the same instant she heard Jason's voice behind them.

"Check in the rest room," he was saying to someone with him. "She should have been back by now."

Beth pulled away from Bram. "I have to get back," she said breathlessly. "Jason is looking for me."

"Let him look," Bram replied, reaching for her again.

"No," Beth said firmly, backing up to the wall. "It isn't fair. I'm his date, and I'm out here with you. . . ."

"Where you prefer to be," Bram finished for her.

"Get out of my way," Beth ordered.

Bram folded his arms, unmoving.

"I mean it," Beth said implacably.

"Oh, all right," Bram said furiously. "Run away. Go back to your dull, safe boyfriend and pretend that he's me."

Beth stared back at him, her lower lip trembling.

"I said go!" Bram repeated, his angry face belying his low tone. "Run away like a scared little mouse and hide from your feelings."

"How dare you say that to me?" Beth demanded, fighting back the threat of tears. "You've been hiding from your feelings all your life."

Bram's eyes widened incredulously. "What?"

"You heard me. You couldn't face what you felt for me the first night we were together so you headed off in the other direction as far as you could get. You bolted for the merchant marine rather than deal with the responsibility of a relationship with a young and innocent girl. You're the coward, Bram, not me."

Bram's face became as hard as granite, his gaze unflinching.

"I needed you to love me," Beth continued unsteadily, "but you turned your back because it was easier and safer. But that's part of your pattern, isn't it? You did the same thing to your father. He needed you, his only son, to stay with him and help him, but you left him when you had some petty disagreements with his wife. He's sick now, and I don't doubt that your abandonment of a lonely old man had a lot to do with that. Do you blame yourself? You should. Don't lecture me about running away, Bram Curtis; you're a master at it."

Bram had gone pale beneath his tan, and his hands were balled into fists at his sides. "You don't know what the hell you're talking about," he said between his teeth.

Beth squared her shoulders. "I think I do," she said quietly. "Despite your macho seafarer act, you're the least courageous person I know. Now, if you'll excuse me, I'll get back to my escort." She brushed past Bram as he remained rooted to the ground.

Jason saw her in the doorway of the room and hurried over to greet her. "I've got everybody looking for you," he said. "Where did you go?"

"I'm not feeling very well," Beth answered. It was the truth. "Do we have to stay for dessert? I think I'd rather go home, if you don't mind."

"Sure," Jason said, in an understanding tone that only made Beth feel worse. "Just wait here. I'll make our excuses and get your shawl."

It seemed an eternity before he returned, but it was only a few minutes. Bram seemed to have vanished; Beth didn't see him anywhere as they made their way outside and the attendant brought Jason's car.

Beth was silent during the trip back to her house, leaning her head back against the rest, emotionally drained. Jason sensed her mood and didn't press to come in with her; he walked her to the door and then said good night, adding that he would call her during the week.

Beth let herself in and walked slowly to the kitchen, running the water in the sink, and then filling a large tumbler and drinking it down. The scene with Bram had been terrible, and she also felt that she had taken advantage of Jason in some vague, undefined way. All in all, it had been a horrible evening, and she wanted only to get into bed and block it all out through the oblivion of sleep.

Marion's door opened as Beth walked past it. She emerged in a cotton nightgown, pushing her hair out of her eyes.

"How did it go?" she asked.

"Not well," Beth sighed, taking off the shawl she was wearing and handing it to her sister. "Not well at all."

Marion yawned. "What happened?"

"I had a fight with Bram."

Marion rolled her eyes. "Now how did I know you were going to say that? I must be psychic."

"Unzip me, please," Beth said. "I can't wait to get out of this dress."

"Do you want to talk about it?" Marion asked, obeying.

"No. That won't change anything."

Marion nodded. "Good. My alarm is set for four A.M.; I have to drive down to Oceanside to pick Jerry up at seven. If I don't get back to bed and start stacking some Z's I'm going to be a zombie when that buzzer goes off."

Beth stepped out of the gown and draped it over Marion's arm. "Thanks for the dress."

Marion's door closed soundlessly as Beth entered her room in her full-length slip and high-heeled pumps. She took off the shoes and stretched out on her bed, not even bothering to undress any further. Feeling exhausted and defeated, she hugged a pillow to her chest and closed her eyes.

In minutes she was asleep.

Beth was awakened by the sound of a distant telephone ringing. She sat up in the dark, confused, listening. Where was it coming from? She had an extension of the house phone in her room, but the instrument on her night table was silent. The ringing came again, insistent, demanding. Beth slid off the bed and made for the door. It was her office telephone on the first floor. By the time she reached the landing she was running.

The grandfather clock in the hall read 3 A.M. Who would be calling on her office phone at this hour? Alarmed, Beth dashed through the door of the office and seized the receiver of the desk telephone.

"Hello?" she said breathlessly.

"Hello?" came from the other end.

"Yes? May I help you?"

"Yeah, well, maybe I have the wrong number. I'm trying to reach an attorney, B. F. Forsyth." The voice was male and querulous.

"This is she."

There was a moment of stunned silence. Then, "Oh. I didn't realize you were a lady."

"Is there something I can do for you?" Beth said impatiently. Why was this clown telephoning her in the middle of the night?

"Yeah, there is, ma'am. I got a client of yours down here in the tank. He had your card in his wallet when we took his personal effects. I thought I would be getting your service at this hour, but since I'm talking right to you, maybe you can tell me what to do."

"Who is it?" Beth asked. But she knew.

"Abraham Curtis. His daddy is some big-deal grower out in the valley. I booked him on a D&D."

Drunk and disorderly, Beth thought. Wonderful. "Who are you?" Beth asked.

"Oh, didn't I say?" the man responded, and then chuckled at his own eccentricity. "This is Sergeant

ENTER THE

*Silhouette
Diamond
Sweepstakes*

WIN The Silhouette Diamond Collection

Treasure the romance of diamonds.
Imagine yourself the proud owner of
$50,000 worth of exquisite diamond jewelry.

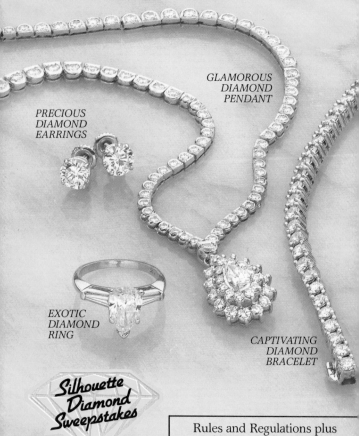

*GLAMOROUS
DIAMOND
PENDANT*

*PRECIOUS
DIAMOND
EARRINGS*

*EXOTIC
DIAMOND
RING*

*CAPTIVATING
DIAMOND
BRACELET*

*Silhouette
Diamond
Sweepstakes*

Rules and Regulations plus
entry form at back of this book.

Canning of the Enfield police. We picked your boy up during a disturbance at the Kit-Kat Club. He wouldn't let me call anybody, but when I found your card I thought I'd take a chance." The sergeant lowered his voice. "He really doesn't belong here, miss, in with all the drunks, dressed in evening clothes like he is. And beat up some, too; he really should see a doctor."

Beth closed her eyes briefly, then opened them. "Will he be arraigned in the morning?"

"Yeah, but he can go home now if you'll vouch for him. It'll be just the standard deal. He doesn't have to spend the night if you can make bail."

"What is it?"

"The set fine, five hundred dollars."

Beth didn't have five hundred dollars in cash in the house. But she knew a bondsman who was open twenty-four hours a day, and she calculated the time it would take her to get to Hartford, and then to Enfield.

"I'll be there in an hour," she said shortly, and hung up.

Marion was sitting on the bottom step of the staircase, her elbows on her knees.

"I woke you again. I'm sorry," Beth said.

Marion turned her palms up. "Who could sleep in this house? What's going on?"

"Bram is in jail in Enfield. I have to drive over there and bail him out."

Marion exhaled slowly. "That guy will never change."

"Maybe so," Beth replied, sidestepping her sister and heading up the stairs. "But the cop said he'd been in a fight. I can't just leave him there overnight if he's hurt."

Marion looked up the stairwell after her. "Are you sure you should get mixed up in this?"

"I'm a lawyer, Marion. I'm just bailing a client out of jail."

"Huh," Marion said expressively.

Beth got a pair of jeans and a shirt from her closet and took them out into the hall, changing as she talked.

"I think maybe this is my fault," she went on quietly. "I said some awful things to him tonight, and I know I upset him."

"So he gets into a dustup because you hurt his feelings. That's very mature."

"I didn't say it was mature. But it's typical of Bram." Beth took her purse and keys from the hall table and hurried down the stairs.

"Don't worry, I'll be all right. Go back to bed," she said to Marion.

Marion made an exasperated face. "The alarm will be going off in half an hour; I might as well just hit the road. I'll be back home around noon if you want to talk."

Beth nodded and waved, sprinting out the door.

Five minutes later she was on the highway, heading for Hartford.

6

Don't you have one of those little plastic cards that you stick into a machine and get money?" the bondsman asked. "My night business is down incredibly since they came out."

"If I had one of those cards, would I be standing here at three-forty in the morning talking to you?" Beth asked.

"Touchy," the man groused. "What are you so worked up about? Five hundred bucks, the charge can't be much. What was your client doing, growing pot in the basement under a plant light?"

"Drunk and disorderly," Beth said shortly.

"Ah. Turned out a bar, huh?"

"Something like that. Could you make it snappy, please, I'm in a hurry."

The bondsman signed the note and slipped it into an envelope, handing both to her. "Lady, next time I get arrested I'm calling you. You do fast work."

Beth smiled weakly, backing out of the door. "Thanks a lot. Good night." She was back out on the street in seconds, gunning the motor of her car toward I91 and Enfield.

The jail was dark except for a single light burning above the door. Beth went inside and discovered Sergeant Canning sitting at the information desk. His name tag was pinned to his uniform blouse.

"I'm Miss Forsyth," she announced to him. "Mr. Curtis's attorney."

The sergeant glanced at her jeans and sneakers. "You don't say."

"Yes, we spoke earlier on the phone. You called me about Abraham Curtis." She handed him the envelope. "Here's his bail."

He nodded, impressed. "That was quick." He removed an accordion folder from a drawer and handed it to her. "These are his personal effects, a wallet, a watch, and some money." He flicked the switch on an intercom at his elbow. "Rafferty, bring up Curtis. He's walking."

Beth shifted nervously.

"Got some ID?" Canning said to her.

Beth showed him her Bar Association card.

"Looks like the ink on it is still wet," Canning observed. "Where did you go to school?"

"Western New England, in Massachusetts."

Canning scratched his graying head. "I got a nephew at U Conn Law School. Wants to do taxes."

"That's very lucrative," Beth said, wondering how long this would take.

"Eh?" Canning said.

"You can make a lot of money doing that," Beth translated.

"Yeah. And you don't have to spend your sleeping time bailing low-lifes out of the clink," Canning replied.

On that note Bram arrived, escorted by a uniformed policeman. Bram was minus his tux jacket, and his shirt was ripped and filthy. There was a large scratch on his cheek, one eye was bruising, and he had what appeared to be a deep cut on his left bicep, bound with a handkerchief. He froze when he saw Beth.

"What's she doing here?" he growled to Canning.

"You're welcome," Beth said sourly.

Canning looked from one to the other, puzzled. "Isn't this your lawyer?" he asked Bram.

"I'm beginning to feel like his mother," Beth said. She surveyed Bram from head to foot. "Look at you; you're a mess. When are you going to grow up?"

"Never," he replied shortly. "I'm Peter Pan."

Beth glanced at Canning. "Is he free to go?" she asked him.

Canning produced a pen and a triplicate voucher. "Just sign for your valuables right here, Mr. Curtis."

Bram scribbled his name, saying to Canning, "I can't tell you how much I've enjoyed my stay in your luxurious accommodations."

"We aim to please," Canning replied, unruffled. He took his pen back and pointed it at Beth. "I'd treat this little lady right, if I were you," he added. "I called her an hour ago and she dropped everything to get here and spring your ungrateful carcass."

Beth lowered her eyes. Bram said nothing.

"Get out of here," Canning said. "Your hearing is 10 A.M., October fifteenth."

Silence reigned as they walked to Beth's car. Bram broke it as she unlocked her door.

"I'll drive," he said.

"You will not. You're in no condition to take the wheel."

She expected an argument, but Bram had apparently had enough conflict for one night. He walked around and got in on the passenger side, doubling up his long legs in the cramped space of the sports car.

Beth slid in next to him, starting the engine. "Your arm looks bad," she said. "We should have it checked out." She snapped her fingers. "I know. Just the job for Dr. Redhead. Or is her practice confined to ankles?"

"Give it a rest, mouse," Bram said wearily.

"How come she wasn't arrested with you? She'll be disappointed that she missed all the excitement."

"I took her home before I . . ."

"Got bombed and tore up the Knick-Knack Club?" Beth suggested.

"Kit-Kat Club," Bram corrected.

"A rose by any other name." Beth downshifted for the entry ramp to the highway. "Call me foolish, call me curious, but might I know what you were doing there? Is that the sort of place you usually hang out?"

"I wanted to get drunk."

"You accomplished your goal."

"I didn't feel like sitting home alone and thinking about what you said to me, okay?"

"Then why didn't you occupy yourself with Dr. Redhead?"

"Her name is Reynolds."

"I don't care what her name is!" Beth yelled. "Or why didn't you call up gorgeous Gloria. I'm sure she'd be willing at all hours. Or that radio station manager. Does she work the night shift?"

Bram's head turned toward her, and even in the darkness she could see the narrowing of his eyes.

"Have you been keeping tabs on me?" he asked.

"Word gets around," Beth answered, uncomfortable.

Bram nodded, as if confirming something to himself. "Melinda Sue Bigmouth," he said. "Otherwise known as the Voice of America."

"Well, you haven't exactly been conducting your affairs in a closet," Beth said defensively. "Of course people are going to talk."

She could feel his gaze on her face. "I wouldn't have a minute for any of them if you'd give me half a chance," he said quietly.

Beth's hands tightened on the steering wheel.

"You know it's true," Bram added. "But you've made it clear that you wouldn't have me if I came gift-wrapped. So what am I supposed to do? Enter a monastery?"

Beth kept her eyes on the road, not answering.

Bram looked out the window, throwing his strong profile into sharp relief as they passed a streetlight. "Bethany, I don't understand you. You want me so much you tremble like a leaf in the wind every time I touch you. You care about me, or you wouldn't have come out at this hour when you heard I was in trouble. Why won't you give us what we both need?"

"You know why," she whispered, still not looking at him.

"Oh, yes," he said in a resolute tone. "Love, or the lack of it. Wonderful love, which makes the world go round, the last best hope of the human race." He gestured dismissively. "It's overrated."

"How do you know? Have you ever been in love?"

"I've seen the behavior of people who said they were in love, and believe me, that was enough." His tone became cynical. "Take my father, for example. A strong, intelligent, capable man. Until he fell in love with darling Anabel. His brains, his strength, his entire constitution went out the window. He became a stupid, fawning weakling, and all for a woman who . . ." he stopped abruptly.

"A woman who . . . ?" Beth prodded.

But Bram was too quick for her. "Never mind," he answered. "Suffice it to say that I can do without an emotion that can transform me into what he became."

"So you've got it all figured out, have you?" Beth asked.

"I think so."

"If you let yourself love anybody, it will diminish you and make you putty in that person's hands?"

His silence was confirmation.

"Then I feel sorry for you," Beth concluded. "You're going to be alone all your life."

"We're all alone all our lives," he replied. "You're kidding yourself if you believe otherwise."

"Is that what you learned in the merchant marine?"

"I learned to take care of myself."

"Oh, I can see that," Beth said tartly. "You did a great job of taking care of yourself tonight."

"Tonight was different," he said defensively.

"I hope so.. I hope you don't make a habit of this sort of thing."

"Give me a break, Bethany," he sighed. "I feel ridiculous enough as it is."

"Are you going to tell me about it?"

He shrugged. She barely saw the movement in the scant light.

"Nothing much to tell. I got tanked and into a fight. Somebody called the cops."

"How did you hurt your arm?"

He shifted uncomfortably. "This guy I hit smashed a beer bottle and cut me with the end of it."

Beth's foot slipped off the accelerator. "What! I'm going to take you to an emergency room right this minute. You could get an infection." She started to pull off onto the shoulder of the road.

"I am not going to any damn hospital," he said with absolute conviction.

"Then maybe we really should call Dr.—"

"If you bring up Althea Reynolds again, I won't be responsible for the consequences," he interjected. His tone dripped icicles.

"All right," Beth responded meekly. "Don't get carried away."

"Can't you take care of it?" he asked, as she pulled back into her lane. "Put iodine on it or something?"

"I hope I won't be putting a Band-Aid on an incision," she said worriedly.

"Nah," he responded. "I've been cut before. This is nothing. I was in a brawl once in Bilbao—some Basque separatist took exception to the fact I was an American. He slashed me with this knife, looked like a scimitar." He stopped abruptly when he noticed Beth's frozen posture.

"Go on," she said evenly. "It sounds fascinating."

He waved the request away. "You don't need to hear any of my boring war stories."

"What a colorful life you must have led during those years," Beth commented, striving to sound unfazed.

"I don't know if 'colorful' is the word I'd use," he said dryly.

"Dangerous?" Beth supplied.

"Only when we were in port. On board ship everything was very routine."

"Nevertheless, you must find life back in Suffield very dull."

"Restful, in a way," he said. "There's only so much high adventure a person can take."

He sounded as if he was teasing, but she couldn't be sure.

"And some of the people at home are endlessly interesting," he said pointedly. "In all the world I've never found others to compare."

That gave Beth a moment's pause. Then she asked, "What about your car? Should we stop and pick it up?"

He shuddered in mock horror. "I wouldn't ask you to go into that neighborhood," he replied. "I'll leave it in the club lot, where it will doubtless be stripped to the ground by morning."

"Should we go to my house?" Beth asked. "I have disinfectant and bandages."

He turned his hands out, palm up, to indicate that it made no difference to him. "I still think you're overreacting."

A thought struck Beth as she turned onto the country lane shared by the Curtis and Forsyth houses. "You know, I think I've gotten more information out of you during the last half hour than I have in the whole rest of the time I've known you," she said, amused.

"You could get information out of a stone."

"But not out of you. Not before tonight, that is."

"I'm a captive audience," he said, only half kidding. "It was either talk or be thrown out onto the road."

"I'm glad you understand the conditions," Beth replied, and he laughed.

She pulled into her driveway and turned off the motor and the lights. "Here we are."

It was the darkest hour of the night, silent except for the sound of a few insects lingering after the summer, and the scampering of small animals in the brush. As they walked together to the front door, Beth realized that they would be alone in the vast, empty house. Her heartbeat increased as she unlocked the door and they went inside.

"Don't you get nervous sleeping here by yourself?" Bram asked, glancing up at the stairwell ascending into darkness.

"I have a security system," Beth explained, shutting off the alarm with a key. "My father had it installed before he died." She shot him a glance. "And of course you're just down the road."

"Too far away to do any good in an emergency," he said grimly.

"I'm used to being on my own," Beth replied, leading the way upstairs.

"Maybe you should get a dog," Bram suggested.

"I don't like dogs. I like cats. I'll get a cat. A guard cat."

"You won't think it's so funny if this place gets robbed," he went on, following her into her bedroom, where she snapped on the light.

"You're turning into a terrible worrywart," Beth said. "I'll be fine." She pointed to her bed. "Sit there, and I'll get the things from the bathroom." She went to search the medicine cabinet for what she wanted.

When she came back into the room Bram was seated gingerly on the edge of the bed, looking distinctly uncomfortable. He didn't like receiving aid from anybody, and especially not from Beth.

He eyed the basin she was carrying unhappily. "Why don't we just forget this?" he said, half standing. "If this arm were going to fall off it would have done so by now."

Beth faced him, her expression implacable. "Sit down," she said in a tone that indicated she would brook no nonsense.

He sat down.

"Let me have a look at that eye," she said musingly, touching the discolored flesh gently. It was bruised.

"You should put some ice on this," she advised. "You're going to have a gorgeous shiner."

He grunted.

Beth washed the scratch on his cheek and swabbed it with disinfectant. "You look like you have war paint on one side of your face," she said, chuckling. "Sort of like a bearded Indian."

"I'm glad you find this amusing," he said darkly.

"If you're going to behave like a little boy, you have to expect to pay the consequences. Now for the arm." She undid the stained handkerchief carefully, then sucked in her breath when she saw the cut.

"Bram, this must be very painful," she said softly.

"I know it's there," he said brusquely.

"You'll have to take off your shirt," she said.

He unbuttoned what was left of his dress shirt and

took it off, slipping it carefully down his injured arm. Beth dragged her eyes away from the spare, hard beauty of his torso, concentrating on the wound.

"I think this may need stitches," she said doubtfully. "It looks awfully deep."

"It's stopped bleeding, hasn't it?" he asked.

"I think so. The blood is all coagulated around the cut."

"Then it doesn't need stitches," he said abruptly. "Just bind it up."

Beth followed his advice, washing the cut and disinfecting it, then bandaging it with gauze and tape. She stepped back finally, admiring her handiwork.

"The skin around it is cool," she pronounced. "I don't think it will infect."

"Thank you," he said quietly. "You should have gone into medicine. You have a very gentle touch."

Beth met his eyes, then looked away. "Let me just adjust it a little," she said, fussing to cover her embarrassment. She reached out to refasten the tape, and then paused, her attention caught by something she hadn't noticed before.

"What's that blue mark on the inside of your arm?" she asked. "It's so small I can hardly make it out."

"Tattoo," he said shortly, pulling his arm away. "I had it done on a dare once in a parlor in Lisbon."

"Let me see," she said, curious.

He stood quickly, moving away from her. "I can't imagine why you're interested," he said. "It was a childish thing to do; I've often thought I should have it removed. I did a lot of silly things in those days. I'm not proud of it."

His attitude convinced her that he was hiding something. "I'd still like to see it," she persisted.

"Oh, all right," he said angrily, turning and thrusting his arm under her nose. "There it is."

Beth looked down, her expression changing as she realized the reason for his reluctance.

"It's a mouse," she breathed, touching it lightly with the tip of her finger. The tiny, perfectly formed animal indented with his skin.

"That's right," he said tightly, yanking his arm out of her reach again. "Satisfied?"

Beth took a few seconds to absorb the import of what she'd seen. "Did you do that," she finally said hesitantly, "because of me?"

"Yes, yes, because of you," he replied furiously. "Why else would I put a damn mouse on my damn arm?"

Beth covered her mouth with her hand. "Oh, Bram."

He stared back at her, his expression unreadable.

"When?" she asked.

"About six weeks after your father's barbecue," he answered quietly. "I couldn't forget you." He suddenly surged forward and took her face between his hands. "Damn you, I never have been able to forget you."

Beth slipped her arms around his lean waist, pressing her face against his bare shoulder as his hands fell away. Hot tears ran from under her lids and stained his skin. He pulled her into the curve of his body convulsively, and she felt his lips moving in her hair.

"Don't cry," he whispered. "Don't cry."

"You didn't want me to see it," she sniffled, turning to kiss his warm, muscular chest. "You didn't want me to know."

His hand bunched in the hair at the back of her

110

neck, and he turned her face up to his. "Don't waste them, mouse," he murmured. "Kiss me on the mouth."

Beth moved before he did, standing on tiptoe to press her lips to his.

He responded with such abandon that Beth realized, for the first time, the effort he'd been making during the past weeks to control himself. Once he found her yielding and submissive in his arms the full tide of his passion was unleashed and engulfed them both.

He kissed her everywhere he could reach, his mouth moving over her face, her ears, her neck. It was as if he was trying to make up for the deprivation of a decade in an instant. His mouth returned to hers, his tongue probing deeply. Beth moaned, returning each caress, unable to resist him any more. He did care about her, she was sure of it now. He might not admit it, but the tattoo on his arm was more of an admission than anything he could say.

"I want you now, tonight," he said huskily, his hands moving under the hem of her shirt, running over her back. "I need you, I want to bury myself in you."

"Oh, Bram, I need you, too," Beth answered, drunk with sensation.

"Do you, baby?" he murmured. "Do you?"

"Yes, I do. I always have."

He pulled the shirt over her head, dropping it on the floor. He bent his head immediately, kissing the satiny surfaces he'd uncovered. His fingers unhooked the latch of the wispy strapless bra she'd worn under Marion's gown, and it fell to the rug, too.

Bram had a nipple in his mouth almost before he'd

seen it, his hand moving to cover her other breast at the same time. Beth gasped and swayed, the delicious friction of his lips and tongue against her sensitive flesh rendering her speechless.

Bram straightened, picking her up and walking to the bed. He set her on it, full length, and then knelt down, unsnapping her jeans and removing them. When she was wearing nothing but her bikini briefs, he put his arms around her hips and pressed his face against the silken skin of her belly.

"Ten years," he whispered. "Ten years I've waited for this." He ran his lips along the edge of her panties, tracing the line of her abdomen, her thighs. Beth's hands clenched on the bedspread. He lifted one balled fist to his mouth, kissing it until it relaxed and opened. He pressed a kiss into the palm, and Beth's fingers touched his flushed, hot face.

"Hurry," she murmured.

He stood and took off his clothes while Beth turned her head, looking away.

"The light," she said. "Turn it off."

"But I want to see you," he protested.

"Please," she said. "I'm shy, I truly am."

He obeyed, flicking the switch on the wall, shrouding the room in semidarkness. Only the glow of the porch light cast a dim pool of yellow across the bed.

Bram dropped beside her, enfolding her immediately. Beth stiffened when she felt the full shock of his naked body.

"What is it?" he said, sensing the change instantly. "You're not afraid? Not of me?"

"Just hold me," she replied. "I just want to feel you next to me and know it's you."

Bram ran his hands down her arms, over her

shoulders, soothing her. "There's no reason to be nervous," he said softly. "I'm always gentle, and I would never hurt you, Beth. Never you."

I should tell him, Beth thought. I should tell him now. But what if he turned away from her and she lost this chance forever? It could only be Bram for the first time. Only Bram, even if they were never together again.

He shifted position, slipping his leg between hers, and she felt the full force of his arousal. She whimpered, caught between desire and fear, unsure of what the next minutes would bring, but at the same time wanting him almost more than she could bear. When he reached down to take off her bikini, she lifted her hips to accommodate him. Then he pressed his palms into her shoulders, pushing her gently backward. Once she was prone, he eased his weight onto her. Beth put her arms around his neck and held him close.

"I never wanted anyone but you," she whispered into his ear. "No other man even came close."

He raised his head and looked into her eyes. There was an expression in them Beth had never seen before, almost akin to pain.

"Oh, Beth, how guileless you are," he murmured. "You have the same sweetness you had when you were sixteen." He kissed her tenderly, his mouth full and soft on hers.

"Make love to me," she said as his lips left her own.

He did so, moving down her body, caressing her with his mouth and hands until she was inarticulate with pleasure. She clutched his arms to bring him back to her, and when he slipped his hands beneath her hips to position her, she was ready.

Bram thrust into her, unprepared for the resistance

he encountered. Beth cried out in pain, and he stopped, shocked, realizing immediately what had happened. He withdrew slightly, lifting her against him, cradling her.

"Oh, baby, why didn't you tell me?" he muttered.

"I thought you might not want me," she whispered.

"Not want you?" His deep voice was incredulous, timbred with emotion. "Of course I'd want you. But I handled you wrong. I thought, I assumed you had experience."

She held onto him tightly, afraid that he might pull away. "Can we try again?" she asked. "I promise I won't make a sound."

He started to shake, and it was several seconds before she realized that he was laughing.

"What is it?" she asked, bewildered.

"You can make all the sounds you want, mouse. I'm looking forward to hearing them."

She sighed with relief. "Then it's okay?"

"It's perfect. You are perfect." He settled her back into the pillows and brushed her damp hair back from her face. "It may hurt again. I'll do my best to go easy."

"I don't want you to go easy," she whispered fiercely, pulling him down on top of her. "I want you to take me, fill me, burn me up." She wound her legs around him, digging her heels into his thighs.

Aroused beyond control, Bram took her at her word.

And in the early hours of the fall morning, as the thin dawn light filled the valley, Beth had her desire.

"Are you all right?" Bram murmured, drawing the sheet over both of them.

"I'm wonderful," Beth replied drowsily.

He was silent for a moment, and then said, "Can I ask you a question?"

She snuggled into his chest and planted a kiss on his collarbone. "You, Mr. Curtis, can ask me anything."

"Why didn't you ever sleep with another man?" he asked.

"No one ever made me feel the way you had, that night we almost made love. I came close a few times, when men pressed me, but I never could go through with it. I always remembered how it was with you, and nothing else could compare."

Bram went very quiet, his body so still he seemed asleep. But Beth could tell by the quality of his breathing that he was still awake.

She sat up, trying to see his face. "What is it? Did I say something wrong?"

He didn't answer, merely pushed her back down into the cocoon of his body. "Shh," he said. "Go to sleep."

Beth settled against him, taking care not to disturb his injured arm. She ran a seeking hand over his heavily muscled abdomen. "Where's the scar from the brawl in Portugal?" she asked.

He took her hand and placed it on his thigh, where she could just feel the thickened ridge of tissue, obscured by the dense mat of black hair. "Right there."

"And what's this?" she asked, touching an uneven mass of flesh on his ribs.

"That's from a burn I got when a boiler exploded," he explained. "The chemical ate right through my shirt."

"I can see I was missing a lot by spending all my time in school," Beth commented.

"You didn't miss anything by skipping those incidents," Bram said quietly, stroking her hair. "They weren't much fun."

"But you've lived life, gone places, seen things. All I've done is accumulate degrees and file court papers."

He chuckled. "Nothing else?"

She smiled. "I did something else just now with you."

Bram tucked a wisp of her hair behind her ear and asked again, "Are you sure you're okay?"

"Of course. What are you worried about? Do you think I'm going to disintegrate?" She tilted her head back and peered at him in the pale sunlight filtering through the window. "Am I the first . . . beginner . . . you've ever been with?"

He didn't answer.

"I am," she said triumphantly. "I knew it!"

He smiled at her victorious tone. "I made it a practice to avoid them after your father threw me out of his house."

That wasn't the reason, Beth thought. He'd only wanted to sleep with women who wouldn't demand, or even expect involvement. That is, until now.

She reached up and touched his face, drawing her fingers through the thicket of his beard. "You're not such a tough guy, after all, do you know that?"

His lips twisted. "I thought I told you to go to sleep."

Beth kissed the base of his throat. "I'm not tired."

He ran his hands under the sheet, seeking her body. "No?"

"No," she confirmed, putting her head back sub-missively as he bent to kiss her.

And she showed him that she wasn't.

When Beth woke hours later the lush sunlight of midday was cascading across the bed, and Sunday quiet filled the house. She sat up, confused, and then remembered. She looked around for Bram, and saw him sitting in a chair beside the window, wearing only his pants.

She got up and found a robe in her closet, slipping into it. She went to him and knelt next to the chair, putting her arms around his waist.

"Good morning," she said. "Or should I say, good afternoon?"

He said nothing, his hand going to the back of her head, his fingers moving slowly through the heavy mass of her hair.

"Would you like something to eat?" Beth asked. "I have eggs, toast, and coffee."

He gently put her hands away and stood up. "No, thanks. I think I'd better be going."

"Are you sure? It's no trouble."

He turned to look at her, and Beth felt a sinking sensation in her stomach at the expression on his face. "Bethany, we have to talk."

"Talk away," Beth said lightly, trying to bluff it out.

He sighed. "I don't know how to say this."

"Just say it straight out," Beth answered. "That's usually best."

"I don't think you should attach too much impor-tance to last night," he said, looking away from her.

"Too much importance?" Beth repeated dumbly.

"Yes," he said. "I was still a little drunk, and feeling

low, and grateful that you helped me out, and you were . . ."

"In love with you," Beth stated flatly.

He tensed. "Don't say that."

"Why not? It's true."

"Beth, you don't have enough experience to make a judgment. You can have fine, satisfying sex with any number of men. Just because we were good partners doesn't mean we're in love."

"You can rationalize it any way you want, Bram. I love you, or I wouldn't have gone to bed with you, and you know it. Don't you love me?"

"I don't love anybody," he said flatly.

Beth stared at him, surprised at her own calm. On some level she must have known this was coming or she wouldn't be able to handle it so well.

"I don't believe you," she said evenly. "You couldn't have made love to me the way you did if you felt nothing. You're talking yourself out of it because you're afraid."

"Afraid?" he said, his eyes becoming hard.

"Yes, afraid. Afraid to give yourself, afraid to become entangled with a woman who might trick you. You were afraid of me when I was a teenager, and you're afraid of me now."

He blinked, and turned his head.

I'm right, Beth thought. I know him, and I'm right. Bram was not a liar; he wouldn't deny the accuracy of her perceptions, but rather take refuge in silence.

Beth moved forward, seizing her advantage. "I think you love me, Bram. I think you always have. You just refuse to admit it, even to yourself, because you think it will make you weak and dependent like your father."

He looked back at her. "I thought your degree was in law, not psychiatry."

"I don't need a degree to figure you out, darling. To me, you're as transparent as glass. You explained yourself last night in the car."

He eyed her intently for a moment, and then dropped his eyes. "Believe what you want."

"I will."

He looked around uncomfortably. "Do you have something I could wear back to the house? My shirt is in rags."

Without a word Beth went to Marion's room and got a shirt of Jerry's that was hanging in the closet. She returned and handed it to Bram.

He put it on, rolling up the sleeves, which were too short.

"I'll drive you home," she said.

"I can walk," he replied shortly, heading for the door. He turned on the threshold and said, "You'll still go on representing Curtis Broadleaf?"

"Of course," Beth said smoothly.

He nodded, studying her once more, looking as if he was about to say something. Then he thought better of it, opened the door, and left.

Beth walked to the window, which looked out over the lawn, and waited for Bram to pass on the street. When his tall, broad-shouldered figure came into view, she watched him, his long stride, the erect carriage of his back and head. When he was out of sight she sat in the chair he had occupied minutes before and thought about what to do.

He wouldn't pursue her any more; she was sure of that. He had accomplished his goal of getting her into bed, but he didn't like the emotions the experience had aroused in him.

Beth tapped her index finger on the upholstered arm of the chair.

But she wasn't giving up on him.

Not by a long shot.

7

Monday was very busy for Beth, and she had to put the subject of Bram on the back burner until dinnertime. She had spent the morning in a hearing on a custody case referred to her by Hal's cousin, and the afternoon doing research on a torts problem involving a company one of her clients wanted to sue. By the time her phone rang at five-thirty she was hungry and tired, but satisfied with the work she'd done.

"Attorney Forsyth," she announced crisply.

"Hi, Attorney Forsyth. This is Mother Crawford-Harris. What's new?"

"Mindy," Beth said, half laughing. "If you call me on this line you have to expect to get the full treatment."

"Hey, I was impressed. You sounded very professional."

"I'm not feeling very professional at the moment. My stomach is growling."

"Feed it."

"I intend to." ·

"And once you do, expect a visit from yours truly this evening. Hal has a zoning meeting and I am hiring a babysitter and fleeing the nest."

"Bad day?"

"You might say so. The baby screamed for four hours and your godchild fed the dinner hamburger to the dog."

"Oh, dear. Well, I'm glad you'll be coming over. I have something to discuss with you."

"Oh, oh. Sounds ominous. Can you give me a hint?"

"Um, let's see. There was a reckless moon out Saturday night."

"I see. That's a big help. Care to elaborate?"

"A reckless moon releases your inhibitions, makes you give vent to your feelings."

"Gotcha. We're talking about Bram Curtis. Sweetie, I can't wait to hear the details, but right now I have to go because Tracy is trying to climb into the sink. See you about seven. Bye."

"Bye." Beth hung up and stretched, trying to remember what was in the refrigerator. She recalled leftover pot roast and a pound of apples. Neither prospect held much appeal. She smiled as she rose to go to the kitchen. Bram's ears would be burning tonight.

Mindy arrived bearing a half gallon of ice cream. She headed directly for the kitchen.

"I thought you were on a diet," Beth said.

"I am. Why do you think I brought it over here to eat? Hal watches me like a Doberman on patrol."

"I shouldn't contribute to your delinquency," Beth said, going to the cupboard for dishes. "What about your self-control?"

"I have no self-control. Give me the bowls."

Beth deposited the crockery on the table and went to a drawer for spoons.

"So what's up with Bram?" Mindy asked, taking a spoon from Beth and digging into the fudge ripple.

"He spent the night here Saturday."

Mindy paused in midscoop. After a moment she said, "Should I be happy about that, or what?"

"Wait until you hear the rest of it. On Sunday he announced that I shouldn't 'attach too much importance' to what had happened; we were just good bed partners, nothing more."

Mindy licked a streak of fudge from her spoon. "Beth, don't take this the wrong way, but surely you don't think you're the first woman who's heard that on the morning after."

"No, I don't. But if you could have seen the way he acted, Mindy, you'd know that this was different."

"How?"

"He's running. He's running because he's in love with me and he doesn't know how to handle it."

Mindy stared at her. "Wow. Nothing wrong with your ego, is there?"

"I'm certain I know what I'm talking about."

Mindy rolled her eyes. "He's a ladykiller, Beth."

Beth slapped her cheek in mock surprise. "No!"

Mindy shot the carton of ice cream across the table to Beth. It flew across the Formica like a puck on ice. Beth stopped it with her hand.

"He's used to one-night stands," Mindy persisted. "You could get hurt if you insist on making it something more in your mind."

"It *is* more. Mindy, you've known him a long time; have you *ever* seen him pursue anyone the way he pursued me?"

"No," Mindy admitted. "But that may have been the lure of the unattainable. You gave him more trouble than usual, that's all."

"Thanks a lot."

"I'm trying to be frank with you. I wouldn't be doing you a favor if I told you fairy tales." Mindy watched as Beth helped herself to some ice cream. "What are you going to do now?"

"Nothing. A good campaigner knows when to retreat."

Mindy groaned. "Where did you get that? Translating Caesar's *Commentaries* in Galsworthy's Latin class?"

"I can read Bram very well. It would be a mistake to push him now; he has to realize how much he needs me, misses me on his own."

"Oh, boy. Watch out. The last time you got that determined look on your face we both wound up suspended for setting all those guinea pigs free."

"I was right then, and I'm right now."

"I feel like calling Bram up and warning him. The poor guy doesn't know what he's in for."

"Whose side are you on?" Beth demanded, outraged.

Mindy held up her hands. "I intend to remain neutral." She clicked her spoon against the side of the bowl. "What does Marion think of all this?"

"She doesn't know about it. I haven't talked to her since before it happened."

"I meant, what does she think of you and Bram?"

Beth snorted. "She's in marriage world with Jerry the stockbroker, perfect husband and perfect man. Bram is about as far removed from Jerry as you can get. Marion hasn't changed since we were kids. She still thinks Bram is bad news."

"If she can't understand your attraction to Bram, she should see a doctor. I don't care how much she loves Perfect Jerry, any woman on earth could appreciate the lure that Bram exerts. He's like some dark, exotic mystery waiting to be explored."

Beth stared at her friend, surprised and touched. "That's it, exactly."

Mindy made a face. "Don't sound so shocked. Do you think because I'm spending my days reading Golden Books and changing diapers that I'm incapable of poetic sentiment?"

Beth grinned, chastised. "Certainly not."

"Anyway, don't be too hard on Marion. She loves you and she tries, but she's just like your father."

Beth shrugged. "Sometimes I think I underestimate her. The other night she asked me if Bram took my breath away. I wouldn't have thought she could even formulate the question."

"It's hard to believe Jerry ever took anyone's

breath away, including Marion's," Mindy observed dryly.

"Jerry's a nice enough guy," Beth qualified hastily, feeling disloyal to her sister. "But he's very straight and conservative. Bram, on the other hand, quit school, joined the merchant marine, and sailed around the world, and now has the scars and the cynicism to show for it. How could a woman who married Jerry Westfield possibly understand him? Marion thinks Bram is wild, primitive, dangerous. She's afraid of him."

"And you?"

"I think he's wild, primitive, dangerous. And I'm crazy about him."

Mindy sighed heavily, closing the carton of ice cream and rising to put it in the freezer. "Well, my friend, I hate to tell you this, but I think you're in for a hell of a time."

"I know that. I won't get him easily, if I get him at all." She met Mindy's eyes squarely. "But I have to try."

Mindy turned from the refrigerator and faced her. "Is there anything I can do to help?"

Beth smiled slyly. "I'm glad you asked that question."

Mindy closed her eyes. "I'm already sorry I said that."

"Do you remember when you told me about Jacinta, the housekeeper who used to work for Bram's father? She's a nurse at Johnson now."

"Sure. What about her?"

"What ward does she work in? I want to go to see it."

"She's in pediatrics, the three to eleven shift. Why do you want to see her?"

"I want to ask her about Bram."

"Good luck. Do you think you're just going to waltz in there and give her the third degree about her former employer's kid? Do you imagine you'll get her to tell all, like one of those lady cops on television?"

"She may talk to me if I tell her the whole story. Everybody says she really liked Bram."

Mindy nodded. "She and your mother were his biggest boosters. He didn't have many."

"Something happened to drive Bram out of his home, and I think it's all tied up with his attitude about women now. He can't trust me—he really has trouble trusting anybody. His stepmother gave him a hard time, and I feel that was the beginning of his problems."

"The beginning of yours, you mean." Mindy leaned back against the refrigerator and folded her arms. "There's no guarantee that Jass knows anything."

Beth pushed her hair back from her face. "She was living in the same house with Bram all those years. She has to know more than I do." Suddenly she sat up straighter. "I forgot to tell you about the mouse tattoo."

"Mouse tattoo?" Mindy said, looking at her strangely. "You mean mouse as in Mickey?"

Beth shook her head emphatically. "No, no, listen. Have you ever heard Bram call me 'mouse'?"

Mindy's brows arched. "Yes, I did notice that. I always meant to ask you why."

"I told him about the time I was one of the dancing mice in the Christmas pageant."

"Yeah," Mindy said, grinning hugely. "You crashed into the tree and knocked off about ten ornaments."

Beth stared at her with exaggerated patience.

"All right, all right," Mindy grumbled. "You were saying?"

"The other night I noticed he had a small tattoo on the inside of his arm."

Mindy shuddered. "I hate those things."

"So does he, apparently. He said he did it on a dare; I got the impression he was with a group and they were all drunk or something. Anyway, it's a mouse."

Mindy's expression changed. "I see. He had it done after . . ."

Beth inclined her head, not letting Mindy finish. "About six weeks after. Doesn't that tell you something?"

"It tells me that you were on his mind, all right."

"That's correct. And he never had it removed, even though he said he'd thought about it."

"Sort of like a brand, isn't it? Like saying, 'This animal belongs to—'"

Beth threw a dishtowel at her.

"It was just a thought," Mindy said, laughing. "Look, much as I dislike changing this intriguing subject, there was a method to my visit tonight. I need to borrow your black beaded purse."

Beth feigned offense. "And here I thought you rushed over to listen to my tale of woe."

"That, too. But I still need the purse. I have to go to a formal with Hal next week, and I'm not going to put myself in the poor house running around buying a bunch of fancy accessories. I can't afford them and I'll never use them again."

"Come on," Beth said, smiling. "I know it's some-where in my room, but it may take some time to find it."

Mindy followed her out of the kitchen. "Time I've got. What I don't have is a black beaded purse."

Laughing, the two women climbed the stairs.

On Wednesday evening Beth drove out to Johnson Memorial at about seven-thirty, thinking that she might catch Jacinta Lopez on her eight o'clock break. Mindy knew another nurse who worked the same shift, and had told Beth that the staff broke for their meal at about that time. Beth had no idea where Jacinta lived, and neither did Mindy. If Beth wanted to contact her at all, she would have to do it at work.

Johnson Memorial was set in a pretty grove of trees on a rural road, and as Beth turned into the asphalt drive leading to the main entrance, she wondered if she was following a blind alley. But she didn't know what else to do. She needed to get some insight into Bram's character and she wasn't going to get it from him.

The woman at the information desk told Beth that pediatrics was on the fourth floor. She took the elevator up to what was obviously a new wing, spotless, with cream-colored tiled walls and a floor that shone with recent waxing. The nurses' station was in a nook at the center of the corridor. She stopped an RN, who was assembling medications on a tray, and asked her where she might find Mrs. Lopez.

It appeared that Mrs. Lopez was doing a treatment in one of the rooms. Disappointed, Beth asked if she could wait to see her. The nurse pointed to a small lounge at the end of the hall and told Beth that she would send Mrs. Lopez down there when she was finished.

Beth waited for ten minutes, leafing through the outdated magazines provided by the management. She was just giving up on an article about refinishing furniture, a subject about as interesting to Beth as terrace farming, when Mrs. Lopez appeared in the doorway, looking at her curiously.

"You wanted to see me?" she asked Beth.

Beth rose, approaching the older woman. She looked unchanged from Beth's memory of her; perhaps the threads of gray in the glossy black hair were new, or the lines etched around her mouth, but she remained the handsome, dignified Hispanic madonna Beth recalled.

"I'm Bethany Forsyth, Mrs. Lopez," Beth said. "Carter Forsyth's younger girl. Do you remember me?"

The woman smiled. "Of course I do now. You look a lot like your mother. You can call me Jass."

"Thank you. I wonder if I could talk to you for a few minutes?"

Jass hesitated, glancing over her shoulder. "I have to get back to the station."

"Aren't you due for your break in a short while?"

Her eyes narrowed. "Yes. How do you know?"

"My friend Mindy told me. She told me you worked here, too."

Jass smiled at the mention of Mindy's name. "That one. Always into everything." Her black eyes flicked over Beth, quick with intelligence. "Why did you want to see me?"

"I wanted to ask you about Bram Curtis," Beth replied.

Alarm crossed Jass's face. "What about Abraham? Is he all right?"

"He's fine," Beth said reassuringly. "But I need to talk to you about him. I know it's a lot to ask, but all I need is a few minutes to explain, and if you don't want to talk after that, I promise I'll go. Can I just wait until you get your break and see you then?"

Jass was silent as she made up her mind. Then she said abruptly, "There's a staff room at the other end of the corridor. Wait outside the door for me. I'll be there as soon as I check back in at the desk and let them know I'm going off the floor."

"Thank you so much," Beth said, relieved. "I'll see you then." She hurried to the appointed spot and waited impatiently for Jass to return.

She did so momentarily, walking soundlessly in her crepe-soled shoes. She gestured for Beth to precede her into the room, which was occupied by two other nurses.

Jass nodded to them pleasantly, and headed for a table across the room from theirs, putting as much distance between them and herself as she could. Beth followed, noticing that they could hardly hear the murmur of voices from the other two people as they sat down. Jass did not want to be overheard.

Jass sat back wearily, sighing, and unpinned her cap, plain white, without the band the registered nurses wore on theirs. She set it on the table between them and leaned forward on her elbows.

"So, pretty Miss Forsyth," she said, her Spanish accent discernible but slight, "what is it you want to know?"

"I want to know why Bram left home at seventeen. I

131

want to know why he quit school and joined the merchant marine to get away."

The woman's eyes flickered warily. "What makes you think I know?"

Beth shrugged. "You were there. Nobody else will talk about it, especially Bram."

Jass shook her head incredulously, as if she couldn't believe Beth's innocence—or nerve. "And you think I will tell you? You think I'll break the confidence of an employer who was good to me, and a boy I cared for, to satisfy your curiosity?" She waved Beth away, using a Spanish word Beth didn't understand. "No, niña," she concluded. "Go home."

Beth panicked as it appeared that she would not be able to penetrate the older woman's wall of silence. "But you must tell me!" she cried. "You're my only hope and it's very important to me, and to Bram."

Jass looked over at the other nurses, who had glanced around at Beth's raised voice. "*Silencio!*" she commanded Beth in a fierce whisper.

Beth got the message. She shut up.

Jass waited until the other nurses were talking again, and then said to Beth, "Why is it so important?"

Beth's eyes filled as she realized that this woman probably had the secret to Bram's past, but instead of giving it up was subjecting her to an inquisition that was getting them both nowhere. She bit her lip, trying to think of the words that might unlock the door to the treasure trove of Jacinta's memory.

"I love Bram," she said finally, opting for plain truth. "I love him very much, and I'm afraid we'll never be together because he can't trust me." She wiped hurriedly at a tear that had slipped from her eyelash onto her cheek, looking away. Why did she have to cry at the most inopportune moments? It was humiliating.

Jass's face softened, and she folded her arms, regarding Beth with tolerant concern.

"Why can't he trust you?" she asked quietly.

"That's what I want you to tell me!" Beth burst out, frustrated, then immediately lowered her voice. To her immense relief, the other nurses got up and, after depositing their trash in a receptacle near the door, left the room.

"I think he loves me, too," Beth went on, more calmly, "but he's resisting the commitment. He told me that loving his stepmother made his father gullible and spineless. I think he's afraid of becoming the same way."

"He mentioned Anabel to you?" Jass asked sharply.

"He didn't tell me much," Beth replied, alerted by the change in Jass's tone. "But he gave me the impression he didn't think she was worthy of his father's love."

Jass snorted. "That's for sure," she said, almost to herself. Rising, she went to a locker at the back of the room, and took out a brown paper bag and a mug with her name on it. She helped herself to coffee from an urn on a table under the outside window, and then brought the sack and the cup back to the table.

"Would you like some coffee?" she asked Beth. "There are paper cups for visitors."

Beth shook her head, waiting tensely for Jass to go on.

"I'll tell you," she said, after taking a sip of her drink. "I have never told anyone, for the sake of the father and of the boy. For the woman," she tossed her head, "I care nothing. I was so happy when I heard she left, I cannot tell you. For years and years I took care of that house and the people, after the mother, wonderful lady, died. God rest her soul. Anabel used to say that the furniture was not dusted, the windows were streaked, the clothes were not clean. No one complained before she came. She wanted me gone, but not for the reason she said." Jass's dark eyes held Beth's. "She was after the boy, and she knew I had seen her."

"After him?" Beth repeated, stunned.

"*Sí, sí, es verdad,*" Jass said emphatically. "She wanted him, she would do anything to get him. She went behind the father, waited until he was away or asleep, and she would approach Abraham. I saw it myself, many times."

Beth swallowed, absorbing it.

"Do you understand?" Jass asked, misinterpreting her silence.

Beth nodded.

"How old was Abraham?"

"Seventeen, when he left," Beth answered.

"But he was big, and handsome. She never left him alone for a minute," Jass went on. "And she was beautiful, long blond hair, the face of an angel. And only, let me see, twenty-five? The age difference was not great, much less than between her and the father. Can you imagine how the boy felt? What was he to do? Go to his father and tell him that his new wife was making advances to his son?" She shook her head. "Abraham would not hurt his father, and I'm not even sure the father would have believed him if Bram *had* told him. He thought the sun rose in the morning only if she gave it her permission, he was so in love with that woman."

"But every woman is not like Anabel," Beth whispered. "How can Bram blame me for what she did?"

Jass shrugged. "That age is impressionable. He never forgot her behavior. It made him suspicious."

"Are you sure about this?" Beth asked, recovering slightly.

"Absolutely," Jass confirmed.

"Anabel initiated it all?" Beth inquired.

Jass looked outraged. "How can you ask such a thing? Bram would never show such disrespect for his father. He is a good boy."

Beth blinked, surprised by the woman's vehemence.

"Do you know why I have this job?" Jass continued, stabbing her forefinger in the air for emphasis. "Because Bram gave me the money for the nursing school tuition. When I was dismissed as housekeeper the boy knew why. He went to his lawyer and got an advance on his trust with his father's permission. He told his father the money was to buy stock, and the father was too obsessed with his wife to check on it. Bram gave all the money to me."

Beth listened, deeply touched.

"And when the father had the stroke, Anabel left. She wanted nothing to do with a sick old man. Bram had to get a nurse, and I told him I would work for nothing, to pay him back. And do you know what he said? He said, 'Stay where you are, Jass, you have a good job with benefits and a retirement plan. I'll get somebody from the nursing service who only wants day work.' And that's what he did."

Beth watched her, impressed with her loyalty and affection for Bram.

"Some say bad things about Bram," Jass said. "They don't know him, and they don't know what he had to go through at such an age. When he wouldn't give in to Anabel she made his life miserable, poisoning the father's mind against him. The boy was trapped in an impossible situation; he saw no alternative but to leave."

"Did he tell you he was going?" Beth asked.

"He told no one. I would have taken him to my house, he knew that. But I don't think he wanted charity. He just wanted to get away. So he signed up, and left me a note. That was all."

Beth was filled with pity for the boy Bram had been, deprived of the father he needed, unable to tell anyone the truth. And everyone has been blaming him all these years for taking off, Beth thought. Including B. F. Forsyth, JD. The unfairness of it made her throat tighten.

"You see why I was so careful with the others here," Jass said. "One of them is a terrible gossip, and even now the story would be news with the family still so prominent. I wouldn't want to hurt Joshua; he was a good friend to me. Before she came, anyway. After that, he was blinded by her, and listened only to what she said."

"I feel awful," Beth said quietly. "I said some terrible things to Bram. I didn't realize how wrong I was. I just assumed he ran out on his father because he was willful and immature, refusing to accept the second marriage."

Jass opened her bag and took out a sandwich. "Oh, he wasn't happy about it, make no mistake. He thought the woman was an opportunist, a fortune hunter, which she was. But he would have endured it but for the other thing. He couldn't handle it." She shrugged. "What boy of that age could?"

Beth reached out and covered the woman's hand with her own. "Jass, thank you so much for telling me. This helps me a lot. Now I know what I'm fighting."

"You won't say anything to him about what I told you?"

"Of course not. I'll just have to show him, with my actions, that I'm nothing like Anabel."

Jass raised her eyebrows. "That will be difficult. Bram likes women—he sees many—but he gives himself to none."

She certainly has his number, Beth thought. "Do you see him now?" she asked Jass.

The woman nodded. "Oh, yes. He drops by, we talk. I have no family, you know; my husband is dead and I had no children."

Beth raised her eyes slowly to Jass's. "Do you think I have a chance?"

Jass smiled slightly. "If anyone does, I think you do."

"Why?"

"Because you care so much."

Beth nodded. If love was enough, she would win.

"Good luck," Jass said as Beth stood up.

That's the second person who wished me good luck with Bram, Beth thought, as she walked out to her car. Mindy first, and now Jass.

They must think she needed it.

When she got home an envelope had been dropped through the slot in her front door. It contained five one-hundred-dollar bills. Bram had returned the bail money she'd paid to spring him from jail.

As she moved to put the empty envelope on the hall table, something fell out of it. It looked like a piece of jewelry. Beth picked it up and held it to the light.

It was a gold charm on a thin, delicate chain, obviously expensive. Diamond chips formed the eyes of a small, burnished mouse.

Beth walked to the phone and dialed Bram's number at home. She couldn't keep it; the gift was far too costly and personal.

A woman answered. Startled, Beth was about to hang up when Bram picked up on an extension.

"It's all right, Gloria, I've got it," he said.

The ubiquitous Gloria, Beth thought. Despite herself, the knowledge of the secretary's presence in Bram's house shot through her like a knife.

"Hello?" Bram barked.

"Bram, it's Beth," Beth said, deciding to go through with it.

There was a silence. Then, "I take it you got the money?"

"Yes, and the charm, too. I can't keep it, Bram."

"Why the hell not?" he demanded.

"It's worth a lot and it makes me uncomfortable. It's not the sort of thing I should accept from a client."

"Is that all I am?" he asked, his tone hostile. "A client?"

"That's all you want to be, Bram," Beth replied quietly. "You got that point across last Sunday."

Bram didn't answer for several seconds, and then he said, "You can turn the tables on me very neatly, counselor. I always seem to forget that about you." He paused, and then added, "Is that why you won't keep the damned trinket? Are you punishing me for walking out on Sunday?"

"You didn't walk out, Bram. As I recall, you left by mutual agreement."

There was an elaborate sigh from the other end of the line. "You never give an inch, do you?"

"I can see why you might think that," Beth replied mildly, smiling slightly at the genuine annoyance in his voice.

"Look, Beth, you're being ridiculous about the charm. I can't take the bloody thing back; I had the jeweler alter it and put in the diamonds."

Beth hesitated, and then said, "All right. It's absurd to go on about it." He was as immovable as a cliff, and she wasn't going to spend the evening wrangling with him.

"I agree," he said smoothly. "There's one more thing."

"What's that?"

"My hearing is on October fifteenth. Are you going with me, or what?"

"It's just a formality, Bram. You really don't need representation."

"I'd like you to come with me," he said stubbornly.

Beth wondered about the reason for his insistence. Was he using the hearing as an excuse to see her, or did he really share the layman's fear of court?

"I'll meet you in the lobby before the 10 A.M. hearing," Beth finally said. "Is there anything else?"

"As crisp as lettuce, aren't you?" he said sarcastically.

Beth thought that one over. He was the one who

had pulled back from their passionate encounter, but now he seemed to resent her taking a more distant attitude toward him. Interesting.

"I don't know what you mean," she replied, unable to come up with anything more original.

"Damn you, yes, you do," he said furiously, and slammed the phone in her ear.

Beth stood with the dead receiver in her hand, unsure if she had scored a victory or fought to a draw. It felt a little more like a victory.

Her moment of triumph was short-lived, however, as she recalled that Gloria would be available to comfort Bram and assuage his frustrations. Beth pictured Gloria in Bram's arms, the recipient of the kisses Beth had tasted, and Beth hung up the phone slowly, feeling slightly ill.

She caught sight of herself in the mirror as she walked through the hall and stopped short. Her face was a study in misery.

Get hold of yourself, she said under her breath. Jealousy is a futile, childish, destructive emotion. Don't indulge in it.

Beth took several deep breaths and felt marginally better. But only marginally.

She took the gold mouse from her pocket and fastened the chain about her wrist.

Maybe it would bring her the luck her friends had wished her.

8

~oooooooooo~

During the next two weeks Beth gently discouraged Jason Raines from trying to develop their relationship beyond the professional stage and concentrated on getting her practice in shape. She was determined to keep busy and avoid thoughts of Bram, but this proved difficult when Mindy called and dropped by at all hours to keep her informed of Bram's activities. Mindy seemed to know everything that was going on around the planet, with a special emphasis on Suffield and Connecticut in particular.

"Bram was at the Blue Dragon with that doctor last night," she informed Beth one afternoon, as she sifted through a stack of Beth's mail.

"I'm sure Gloria will be very unhappy to hear that," Beth replied mildly.

"You don't look too pleased at the news yourself," Mindy said bluntly, unpersuaded by Beth's meticulous disinterest.

"He's free to do whatever he wants," Beth said.

"I don't think your plan is working," Mindy offered.

"Give it time."

Mindy's mouth fell open. "Give it time! Beth, he's out with a different woman every night. I wouldn't say he's exactly pining away, would you?"

"He's doing precisely what I expected him to do."

"Oh, really?" Mindy said skeptically.

"Really. He's not the type to moon around and feel sorry for himself. He takes his mind off his problems by going out and keeping himself occupied."

"He's been occupied, all right. By that standard, he must be madly in love with you," Mindy observed darkly.

"Did you come by just to cheer me up, or what?" Beth asked.

"I came by to tell you I hope you know what you're doing," Mindy answered.

"I hope I do, too. But I see no alternative. Am I supposed to join the ranks of Gloria, Althea, et al? The line forms on the right. No, thanks."

"Who's Althea?" Mindy asked curiously.

"That's Dr. Reynolds's first name," Beth replied patiently.

"Sounds like an opera singer," Mindy said, sniffing.

"And looks like a movie star," Beth added sadly.

Mindy sighed. "I guess there's no chance she's stupid, either."

"No chance at all. She's head of the orthopedic service at Johnson."

"Jeez," Mindy said. "That's demoralizing." She held an envelope up to the light. "Are you interested in a subscription to *Barrister* magazine?" she asked Beth.

"Nope."

Mindy threw the envelope in the trash. "When are you going to see Bram again?"

"His hearing is tomorrow. I'm going to meet him at the courthouse."

"Haven't you been working with him at Curtis?"

"I've sent some things over by messenger. I felt if I saw him in person I might do something I'd regret later, so I've been steering clear of him."

"So tomorrow is the big test?"

Beth shrugged. "It shouldn't be too bad. We'll both stand up in front of a judge who will tell Bram what a bad boy he's been. Bram and I won't even be alone together."

"You have four overdue books at the Suffield library," Mindy announced, reading from a slip in her hand.

"Oh, God. I've had them out since the Flood. It would probably be cheaper to buy them than to pay what I owe." She threw down her pen in frustration. "It would take a team of accountants to untangle these records. I need a secretary."

"Get one."

Beth stared at Mindy. "Melinda Sue, I can't afford a secretary."

Mindy brightened. "Hal knows somebody at work whose wife is looking for a part-time job. Maybe you could pay her by the hour, keep the cost down."

"Do you think so?" Beth asked, interested.

"You'll never know unless you try. I'll give Hal your number to pass on, and she can call you."

"Thanks a lot."

"*De nada*," Mindy replied, showing off her high-school Spanish. "Hey, what's this? Looks like a wedding invitation."

"It is. My second cousin Eleanor is getting married."

"Nice paper," Mindy commented, fingering it. "Are you going to go?"

"I guess."

"By yourself?"

"Unless I ask Jason, but I think that would encourage him too much."

"What's wrong with that? Why should you sit home while Bram has a good time?"

"It wouldn't be fair to Jason. I'm not interested in him."

"Then ask Bram."

Beth's eyes widened. She put her hands on her hips.

"Okay, okay, don't listen to me. Nobody else does." Mindy tore up an advertising circular and threw it out. "By the way, did I tell you that Anabel Curtis has a new boyfriend?"

Beth tried not to show a betraying amount of interest. "Who told you that?"

Mindy waved her hand to indicate a variety of sources. "Somebody went to visit her in Florida and brought back the news. It seems some younger guy is living with her. That should make it easier for Joshua to cut her loose, if he wants to."

"Mindy," Beth said thoughtfully, "what did you

think of Anabel? When she was living at the Curtis house, I mean?"

"I hardly knew her. I remember that she was beautiful; that's about it."

"Did you ever hear any talk about her and Bram?"

"The talk was that they hated each other," Mindy answered, drawing her mouth down at the corners. "Why? What did you mean?" she inquired, when she saw Beth's dissatisfaction with her reply.

"Oh, nothing," Beth said evasively, standing up and stretching. "The rest of this will have to wait. I've had enough for one day."

Mindy stood also, glancing at her watch. "I've got to run. Hal will be back with the kids in half an hour." She picked up her jacket and purse, calling over her shoulder, "Let me know what happens at the hearing."

"I promise I won't let them take Bram away in chains," Beth said, grinning.

Mindy chuckled as she went through the door, and Beth heard her car start outside seconds later.

What would it be like, Beth wondered, to be married and settled, with a couple of children? What would it be like to be married to Bram, with Bram's children?

She shook her head quickly, refusing to entertain the fantasy.

She would see him in the morning and, for the time being, that would have to suffice.

The courthouse building was a modern brick structure set incongruously amongst a stand of maples in the old, historic part of Enfield. It looked as if it had been dropped from an airplane to land between the ivy-covered facade of the country day school and the frame and gingerbread outlines of the township of-fices. Beth adjusted the lapels of her wool blazer as she walked up the path to the front entrance. The day was crisp and cool, full of the brisk fall scent of burning leaves and sun-washed apples. On such a day you could almost feel the "breath of autumn's being" sweeping through the Connecticut Valley, and Beth wished she didn't have to spend it indoors.

People milled about the lobby, shuffling papers, examining the copies of the court calendar displayed on the walls. Beth spotted Bram lounging against the balustrade that encircled the staircase leading to the upper floor. He straightened when he saw her, and Beth's pulse leaped at the exact second his eyes met hers.

He waited in silence as she walked toward him, watching her progress across the hall. He'd gotten a haircut, and his beard was trimmed. He was attired in a neat blue suit, and Beth was touched by his efforts to appear respectable. At the same time, she had to admit they were a partial failure; there was a dashing, almost disreputable quality about Bram that even a haircut and a Wall-Street outfit couldn't dispel.

"I missed you," he greeted her, in a voice so touched with quiet sincerity that Beth halted in her tracks.

His dark eyes held hers, anticipating her response.

"I think we should go in and wait to be called," she said. "They usually run a little late, so we'll just sit in the back, all right?"

He hesitated, as if about to say something, and then nodded, indicating that she should precede him. Beth led the way to Room Three, where they were third on the morning's docket.

Beth didn't know the judge, whose name was Worthington, but it was clear that Bram did. He swore expressively under his breath when he saw the man sitting behind the desk, listening to the case that preceded theirs.

"What's the matter?" Beth whispered, turning to look at Bram as they took their seats.

"I had that judge a few years ago when I was here on a disturbing-the-peace charge," he replied shortly. "I was home on leave, at a friend's house."

"What did you do?" Beth asked, concerned.

"Loud party," he said. "Some neighbors called the cops."

"Don't worry about it," Beth assured him. "He sees hundreds of people a month."

"I argued with him," Bram said uneasily. "I don't think I made a very good impression. I sure hope he doesn't remember me."

Judge Worthington remembered Bram. He peered over the tops of his half glasses as Beth and Bram stood before him.

"Mr. Curtis, is it?" he asked, looking down at the papers on his desk.

"That's right," Bram said, his tone tinged with hostility.

Beth kicked him on the ankle.

"Yes, sir," he amended.

"Your honor," Beth hissed.

"Your honor," Bram repeated, looking angry already.

"Ah, yes, Mr. Curtis," Judge Worthington went on, practically rubbing his palms together with anticipation. "I recall your presence before this bench some time ago. Something about playing the bongo drums on the front lawn at two in the morning, wasn't it?"

"Yes," Bram replied stiffly.

"Well, Mr. Curtis, it seems like you've been up to your old tricks again. I have before me a remarkable document detailing your activities on the evening of September twenty-sixth. It appears you were quite busy."

Bram kept silent, obviously feeling that such a lily needed no gilding.

"Unless I'm mistaken, you did us all the great favor of staying out of town for a number of years. Once back, it looks like you're making up for lost time."

Beth could practically see the steam rising from Bram's ears. She shot him a look that told him to hang on to his temper and let the judge needle him. It would all be over soon.

The judge picked up a sheaf of papers and waved them in the air. "This is the police report submitted by our estimable Sergeant Canning, and it's really too good to keep to myself. For the benefit of counsel," he glanced at Beth, "I'll read it aloud."

Bram began to look slightly ill.

"Your name is . . . ?" the judge said, studying Beth.

"Bethany Ferryman Forsyth," she said briskly, in her best professional manner.

"You're new at this bar," he observed. "Any relation to Carter Forsyth?"

"His daughter."

"Hmmph," Worthington said. He looked at Bram. "I can't imagine how you persuaded this lovely young lady to represent you."

Bram's fists clenched at his sides.

The judge adjusted his glasses. "At about eleven forty-five P.M. on the evening of September twenty-sixth, you entered into an altercation with a Mr. Matthew Titus of Thompsonville, Connecticut. According to this report, Mr. Titus was having a drink with friends at the Kit-Kat Club in Enfield, Connecticut, when you entered and sat at the bar. Mr. Titus made a remark about fancy dudes in tuxedos, which you overheard. You responded with an observation about filthy slobs in overalls. Mr. Titus then yelled that you needed a haircut, to which you replied he needed a bath."

The judge paused and looked at Beth, to see her reaction to the recital. Beth kept her expression carefully blank.

"Eyewitnesses stated that both you and Mr. Titus were intoxicated. Mr. Titus had been drinking for a while, and you were inebriated when you entered the bar. Is that so?"

Bram grunted.

"Is that a yes or a no, Mr. Curtis?"

"Yes," Bram growled.

"I see. A pity we couldn't add a drunk-driving charge to those listed here."

"I didn't drive while I was drunk," Bram said. "I had been drinking in the place across the street, and just walked to the Kit-Kat."

"Very admirable," the judge said sarcastically. "It seems that it's only your own safety you have no regard for."

When the judge glanced down again, Beth reached for Bram's hand and squeezed it quickly. He didn't look at her.

"To continue," the judge said, "Mr. Titus threw a

punch at you when you observed that he needed a bath. You ducked it. He swung again, at which point you hit him with a chair."

The judge looked up, taking off his glasses. "It goes on in the same vein, with you making speculative remarks about Mr. Titus' ancestry, and the probable fact that his mother was not married when he was born. Mr. Titus ended the fracas by smashing a bottle and slashing you with it. The police arrived at this juncture and broke up the fight." Worthington folded his arms. "Well, Curtis, what do you have to say for yourself?"

Bram stared back at him stonily.

"Is this account accurate?" the judge asked.

"Substantially," Bram replied.

"What does that mean?"

"It means that Titus started it," Bram replied heatedly. "I tried to ignore him, but he wouldn't let it go."

"It's immaterial who started it, Mr. Curtis. This isn't an elementary-school playground fight we're talking about. You, or Mr. Titus, could have been seriously hurt."

"My client was hurt," Beth interjected. "He sustained a wound on his arm inflicted by Mr. Titus. Has Mr. Titus been charged with assault?"

"You let me worry about Mr. Titus, counselor," the judge said to Beth. "I assure you we have him well in hand. Can we expect this type of behavior from you in future, Mr. Curtis?" the judge asked.

"No."

Beth believed him. During Worthington's monologue he'd looked as if it would be a long time before he touched anything stronger than tea.

The judge fixed Bram with an icy stare. "One could

have hoped realistically that you might have outgrown this sort of thing by now, Curtis. I should give you the two weeks, but for the sake of your father, whom I have known for many years, and who is a respected member of this community, I'll go with the fine this time. But if I ever see your face come before this bench again, you will be cooling your heels in the lockup, make no mistake about it." He banged the gavel. "Seven hundred fifty dollars and six months' probation. Pay the clerk. Dismissed."

Bram turned on his heel immediately. Worthington looked at Beth.

"Counselor, see what you can do to control this wild man, will you?"

"I'll do my best, your honor," Beth replied meekly, and fled.

Out in the corridor, Bram leaned his head back against the wall, pulling his tie loose from its knot. "Whew," he said wearily. "That turkey really raked me over the coals."

Beth nodded sympathetically. "He had it in for you, all right. That kind of hearing is usually over in five minutes with a slap on the wrist and a warning to behave. I don't know why he felt he had to read all that stuff out loud."

Bram turned to look at her. "He was trying to make me look ridiculous, humiliate me in front of you. And he succeeded."

"Oh, Bram, that isn't true," Beth said softly, her heart going out to him. "Everybody makes mistakes."

"Not as many as I make." He glanced away, his dark eyes bleak. "And I keep making the same one." He looked back at Beth, attempting a smile. "You must think I'm a real jerk."

"No, I don't," Beth replied, trying to keep the emotion out of her voice. "I think that you're . . ."

"What?" he prompted, eyeing her intently.

"Unhappy," she finished, watching his reaction.

He smiled grimly, then half laughed as he responded, "God knows, that's true enough."

Beth felt his confusion, his pain, and wished that she could solve everything for him, take away the bad experiences that had made him what he was. But she loved what he was, and was willing to take the bad with the good.

Bram raked his hand through his hair, lifting it from his forehead. "It's my own fault, mouse. The judge was right. I should have outgrown this nonsense; I'm too old to be getting into fights in bars." He grinned suddenly, displaying a flash of the charm Beth found so irresistible. "In fact, I was too old for it at eighteen. That never stopped me, though."

"I feel responsible," Beth said quietly. "I gave you a hard time the night you wound up at the Kit-Kat. Some of the things I said were very unfair."

"Some of the things you said were perfectly true," Bram countered, admiration creeping into his tone. "Told me off, didn't you, counselor?"

"I'm not proud of what I did."

"You should be. Never be ashamed of honesty, not with me, anyway." He smiled slightly. "I might not like hearing it at the time, but I like lies a lot less." He reached out and ran a strand of her hair through his fingers. "Maybe I need an honest woman to make a man of me."

"You're already a man, Bram," Beth answered, afraid to say anything more.

He snorted. "Physically, sure, but I'm not certain

about emotionally." He shot her a sidelong glance. "You see, mouse, I *am* aware of my shortcomings. I just can't seem to figure out what to do about them."

Let me help you, Beth wanted to say. "I think you're all right," she said lightly, half kidding, trying to tease him out of this confessional mood that was bringing her dangerously close to tears. Bram in a rage was at least familiar; this was heartbreaking.

"I think I really could shape up, you know, if I had someone to depend on, someone who would be faithful," he said, almost to himself, as if she hadn't spoken.

I'm here, Beth thought. But he didn't believe such a woman existed, and she knew it. It hurt her deeply that even after their night together he couldn't see that what he needed was standing right in front of him.

A couple passed next to them, laughing, and they both looked up, startled. They had forgotten where they were.

"You look lovely in those clothes," Bram said suddenly, changing the subject. "Like an autumn leaf."

Beth was wearing a rust-and-brown tweed suit with a harvest-gold blouse. "I'm glad you like them," she said.

"And you're wearing my bracelet," he added, delighted. He had caught sight of it when she moved her hand.

"Yes."

He set his hands on her shoulders and turned her to face him, putting her back to the hall.

"Beth, something has been bothering me. The night we spent together—we didn't use any precautions. You could be pregnant."

153

"I'm not."

"Are you sure?"

She nodded.

He seemed not relieved, but almost disappointed, an odd reaction from a man who had made a lifetime fetish of avoiding responsibility.

"Will you have lunch with me?" he asked, still holding her.

"I can't, Bram. I have to meet a client in town."

"So that's it?" he said. "You just go off to your meeting and I don't see you anymore?"

"You'll see me on business in your office."

"That's not what I mean." He released her, stepping away. "How can you be so distant with me after what we shared?"

"That was your choice, Bram, not mine," Beth replied quietly.

He nodded slowly, looking away. "It must be obvious, even to you, that I don't know what I'm doing," he said.

"It's obvious that you have to make up your mind what you want."

Bram continued to look past her, his eyes distant. "And you won't wait forever, will you?" he finally said.

Beth didn't answer, thinking that she probably would.

His eyes returned to hers. "You are one classy lady, do you know that? I took from you the most precious gift a woman has to offer, and then left with hardly a word. And you handled it like a champ: no tears, no recriminations, just the most perfect example of style and grace I've ever seen." He shook his head. "Why did I walk away?"

"You have to answer that for yourself."

He bent his head, jamming his hands into his pockets. The doors of Room Two swung open behind them and disgorged a flood of litigants.

"I'll go," Bram said, looking up, "and let you get to your lunch. Thanks for going with me. You kept me from blowing up and getting into worse trouble."

"Good-bye," Beth said, watching as he blended into the crowd and finally vanished through the door.

He's turning to me, Beth thought, as she walked to the desk to file his disposition papers. He talked to me, and told me what he was really thinking. No more tough line about everyone being alone and learning to take care of yourself. He had shared a little of his mind with her, and she knew that with Bram that was a far more important portion than his body.

Beth nodded to another lawyer with whom she had a passing acquaintance, and then handed in her paperwork. She signed the register, then looked at her watch. Plenty of time to get into Suffield to meet her lunch date.

As she snapped her purse closed, the golden charm she wore flashed with a glint of diamonds.

She smiled, and headed for the door.

9

Two days later the phone was ringing as Beth let herself into her house. She put down her overnight case and dropped her purse on the hall table, hurrying to answer it.

"All right, all right, I'm coming," she muttered, picking up the receiver. She cradled it between her neck and shoulder and bent to remove her shoes.

"Hello?" she said breathlessly.

"Beth!" Marion's voice was urgent. "Where on earth have you been?"

"I went to Boston, Marion, I told you about it. My old boss referred a case to me and I went up there to discuss it with him. Why? What's the matter? You sound like you thought I went to Japan."

"I did. I've been trying to reach you. When are you going to get a secretary, or at least a service to take messages?"

"I just bought a machine, Marion, give me a break. You act like I'm made of money. Are you going to tell me what this is about?"

There was a pause. Then, "Bram's father had another stroke."

Beth sank slowly into a chair. "How bad is he?" Beth asked.

"Not good. Bram was looking everywhere for you last night; he even called me, which is an indication of how desperate he was to find you."

"Oh, God," Beth whispered. Why did this have to happen the minute she left town? "Is Bram at the house?" she asked Marion.

"Yes. He's got a private-duty nurse there around the clock. He's in rough shape, Beth. He really sounds like he needs you." Marion cleared her throat. "It amazed me how broken up Bram was about it. I never thought he cared much for his father."

Beth closed her eyes. Marion didn't understand Bram at all. No one does, Beth thought. No one but me.

"Marion, I have to go. I'll get right over there. Thanks for calling." She hung up before Marion could reply, reaching for her shoes again. She grabbed her purse and ran out the door.

The Curtis house was one of the most impressive in the valley. It was a two-story colonial with a front veranda running the length of the house, supported by tall columns, which gave it the look of a Southern plantation house. A long drive led up to it through rows of oaks standing like sentinels on either side. In the distance Beth could see the first of the tobacco barns that stretched along the landscape for miles. The harvest was in now, and the leaves were drying, tacked to the doors of the sheds. These flipped upward like the pages of a stenographer's notebook, exposing the green leaves to the parching sun. To the right were the buses used to carry the pickers to and from town, still and silent now, parked at random like the discarded toys of a child who had outgrown them. Beth drove into the paved semicircle that faced the house and got out, noticing the presence of several unfamiliar cars. There were others inside besides Bram.

The nurse answered the door. "May I help you?" she said politely, looking Beth over with detachment.

"I'm Beth Forsyth, I live down the road. Mr. Curtis has been asking for me."

The woman's demeanor changed immediately. "Of course," she said, taking Beth's hand and pulling her inside. "Mr. Curtis has been very upset. But he won't talk to me; I don't know what to do for him."

"How is his father?" Beth asked, noticing the hushed, almost expectant atmosphere of the house, indicating the presence of an invalid.

The nurse raised her brows. "The doctor is with him now. I can't say. He seems aware of what's going on around him, though."

"That's good, isn't it?" Beth asked eagerly.

"He can't talk, miss," the nurse added flatly.

"At all?" Beth said, alarmed.

The nurse shook her head. "And his son has been crazy. He threw the cleaning woman the agency sent over right out of the house, said she was making too much noise. And he was asking for you all the time, sent that young lady to look for you."

"What young lady?"

"Short, blond, with a little girl."

Mindy. "Is she still here?"

"No, she had to leave. She said to tell you, if you arrived, that she would call later."

"Is Bram alone? Where is he?"

"In the library, miss. He said not to let anyone in but you."

"I'll go and see him," Beth said, walking past the nurse, and then stopping. "I'm sorry, forgive me. What is your name?"

"Mrs. Harkness."

"Hello, Mrs. Harkness. Thanks for filling me in. Do you know Mrs. Lopez? She's a practical nurse on pediatrics at Johnson."

"No, miss. I don't work out of the hospital; I get my assignments from my agency."

"Oh, I see. I'm glad you were able to help out here."

Mrs. Harkness nodded. "He's very much alone, isn't he?" she asked. "The son, I mean."

"Yes," Beth whispered. "But he wants it that way."

"I don't know about that," the woman said wisely. "He wanted you here, miss."

Beth patted Mrs. Harkness's hand. "Thank you for saying that. And please call me Beth. I'll see you later." She made her way through the deep entry hall, recalling the layout of the house, unable to remember the last time she'd been inside it. The library was at the back, behind the living room, and Beth noticed the change in decor. Bram's mother had favored antiques and family heirlooms, and after she died the men had kept it pretty much as she'd left it, until the advent of Anabel. Now the furniture was stark and modern, chrome and glass, which did not go well with the style of the house or its male occupants. It looked as if it had been done by a decorator, and Beth could well imagine what Bram thought of it. Obviously he had been too busy with the business and his father's ill health to do anything about it since Anabel's departure. But her choice had been an effective one; the memory of Bram's mother was muted almost into silence.

Beth halted outside the closed library door. She knocked. There was no response, so she turned the knob and pushed it inward.

The room was dark, but even so it was obvious that Anabel's modernization project had made no inroads here. Someone had insisted on leaving the place alone, and it was as Beth remembered it, filled with books and plaques, trophies and family pictures, much like Beth's father's den at home. There was a large portrait of some Curtis ancestor over the fireplace, mounted in a heavy gold frame. Beth looked around the room, which appeared to be empty, and would have left except that she caught the strains of music coming from the stereo standing in a corner. It was Debussy's "Afternoon of a Faun."

"Bram?" she said softly. "Are you in here?"

He stood, peering at her through the gloom. He'd

been slouched in an armchair behind the rolltop secretary, hidden from view. "Beth?" he said hoarsely.

"Yes, it's me."

"Beth," he repeated, coming toward her across the room. He caught her in his arms and held her silently, dropping his head to her shoulder.

"I came as soon as I heard," she said. It was strange; he was so much bigger, but she felt as if she were cradling him, comforting him.

"I tried to find you," he mumbled.

"Yes, I know. I'm sorry. I was away overnight on business. I talked to the nurse, Mrs. Harkness. She's very nice, Bram. She says your father is aware of everything, and I've heard that's a very good sign."

He raised his head and looked at her, his eyes bleak. "He can't talk and he can't move his left side at all. It's much worse than the first stroke. I don't need a doctor to tell me that."

"He can have a therapist for that, Bram. They can work wonders."

Bram pulled free of her. "He's had a therapist all this time, and look where it got him. The doctor isn't sure if he'll make it through the night."

"But if he does? Isn't there a chance he'll recover?"

Bram shrugged despairingly. "That's what they say. But what do they know? They thought he was doing fine; that's what they kept telling me. And look what happened."

"Did you find him?"

Bram nodded. "The nurse had left for the day. I came home late and went upstairs to check on him. He was lying on the floor next to the bed." He swallowed and looked away. "God knows how long he was there."

"Bram, that wasn't your fault."

"I left him," Bram said softly, not listening. "I left him alone too long."

"That isn't true," Beth said evenly. "The most it could have been was a couple of hours."

Bram shook his head. "No. I meant when he got married again. I never should have left him alone with her."

Beth didn't know what to say.

"You were right," he added softly. "I ran away. You said it, and you were right."

"Bram, that doesn't matter now," Beth said desperately, wishing that she could call back the hurtful words, trying to steer him away from such painful territory. She was afraid she might reveal that she knew too much about the real reason for his departure.

"I never did it," Bram muttered.

"What?"

He looked down at her, his eyes distant. "Remember when you told me to talk to him, straighten things out between us? I never did it, and now it may be too late."

"It isn't too late. You'll still be able to talk to him, you'll see."

"There are things he doesn't know, things he doesn't understand," Bram went on, almost to himself. Beth knew he was talking about Anabel. "And I can never tell him."

"Then tell him that you love him," Beth said quietly.

Bram turned his head away. "I can't say it," he whispered.

Beth choked back tears. His pain was so palpable she could almost touch it herself. How awful to feel something so deeply and yet be unable to express it. Bram was trapped in the prison of his own silence.

"Yes, you can," Beth urged. "When the doctor says it's okay go up and talk to your father."

Bram pushed his hair back in that characteristic gesture, not answering. After a moment he said, "I was always such a disappointment to him. He wanted me to go to college, get a business degree, take over Curtis Broadleaf." He laughed bitterly. "I didn't even graduate high school. Did you know that I'm the first son in four generations never to attend college?"

"Bram, don't torture yourself about this now. It won't do any good."

"I was always in trouble, an embarrassment," Bram continued. "I even screwed up the one thing I was good at that he liked, sports. He was proud of that. See all these trophies?" he said, making a sweeping gesture around the room. "They're all mine. Most valuable player, conference champion, halfback of the year. But I had to get thrown off the team. I had to ruin that for him, too."

"That was all a long time ago," Beth said wildly, trying to stem the flood of remembrance. But she knew that it was useless. Bram had stored all this up for years, and his father's closeness to death had broken the dam and unleashed it.

"It was because of her," Bram said viciously. "Even that was because of her."

"Who?" Beth asked.

"The coach made a remark about my stepmother," Bram said softly. "He said my father was old, and I might be more to her taste. She was young, and so was I."

Beth held her breath.

"I punched him," Bram said. "I let him have it, and got thrown off the team. I had a chance at a scholarship, but I blew it. And all because of that scheming, money-hungry witch."

There was a knock at the door. Bram turned away, and Beth went to answer it.

It was the doctor.

"Is he worse?" Bram asked dully, not looking at the man.

"No, not at all. He seems alert. Would you like to see him?"

Bram looked at Beth. She nodded, pushing him gently toward the door. Bram took a deep breath, and then brushed past the doctor into the hall.

Beth sat down hard, feeling as if she had just run a race. What a well of feeling lay beneath Bram's hard facade. She hoped she had given him the right advice. A bad experience with his father now would ruin him. She said a silent prayer that everything would go well upstairs, and then looked up to find the doctor staring at her.

"Do you think Mr. Curtis should be taken to a hospital?" Beth asked him.

"No, I don't want to move him. Mrs. Harkness can look after him here, and I'll drop back tomorrow morning. Please tell Abraham that."

Beth nodded, and he slipped out. She got up to shut off the stereo, which was still playing softly, and heard the phone ringing elsewhere in the house. A few seconds later Mrs. Harkness appeared.

"The telephone is Mrs. Harris, for you."

Beth followed the nurse into the hall, asking her, "Is Bram still with his father?"

"Yes."

Beth picked up the receiver as Mrs. Harkness walked away. Silence descended again as her footsteps faded.

"Hello, Mindy," Beth said.

"I see Marion finally found you," Mindy greeted her.

"The phone was ringing as I came through the door."

"How are things there?" Mindy asked.

"Pretty shaky. What time did you leave?"

"Several hours ago, around four this afternoon, I guess. Jass Lopez was there, too, before Mrs. Harkness came. Jass is crazy about Bram, you know."

"I know."

Mindy snorted. "Typical Bram. He acts like a raving maniac most of the time, and what's the result? Half the female population of Connecticut follows him around in a trance."

"He doesn't act like a maniac," Beth said defensively.

"Of course he does. It's just that the rest of the time he's so charming that it doesn't matter."

"Mindy, did you call me up to tell me this?"

"Sorry. How's Joshua?"

"The doctor seems to think he's a little better now."

"And Bram?"

"Not so hot. He looks terrible."

"So what?" Mindy said. "Even when he looks bad, he looks good."

"I mean it, Mindy. I'm worried about him."

"Worry about yourself," Mindy replied tartly. "Underneath the looks and the temperament Bram got from his mother is the steel spine he inherited from Joshua. Bram will survive."

"You don't sound very sympathetic. His father could be dying."

Mindy sighed loudly. "I am sympathetic, Beth. It's just that I don't have the tolerance for his moods that you do." There was a pause. "But then, I'm not in love with him."

And you don't know the whole story either, Beth thought.

There was a muffled commotion on the other end of the line. Mindy covered the mouthpiece and said something, and then returned to Beth.

"I have to go," she announced. "Tracy has recently decided that there is a monster in her closet, so every night at bedtime I have to stand attendance and turn on all the lights. By the time she goes to sleep it looks like we're shooting a movie in her bedroom."

Beth chuckled. Trust Mindy to supply some very welcome comic relief. "Okay. I'll be in touch."

"Give me a call if you need anything," Mindy said, and hung up.

Beth wandered back to the library, turning on a light to alleviate the darkness. She heard a pattering on the roof, and drew aside a curtain to look outside. It had begun to rain.

There was a sound behind her and Beth turned to find Bram leaning against the far wall, his eyes closed.

He looked spent and somehow thinner, as if the day's ordeal had wasted him physically as well as emotionally. He had pulled at his hair so much that it stood up in cowlicks all over his head, and the tail of his shirt was out, draped over his jeans like a referee's flag. His arms hung limply at his sides.

"Bram?" Beth said softly.

His eyes opened.

"Did you talk to him?"

"Yeah." It was an exhalation more than a word.

"What did you say?"

"What you told me to say," Bram replied simply.

"Did he understand you?"

Bram nodded.

"How do you know?"

"He cried," Bram said. "He just lay there, as still as a statue, and the tears rolled down his face."

Beth took a step toward him, and he came the rest of the way. He held her a long time before he said, "What's that sound?"

"It's raining."

Bram released her and walked to the French doors, which opened onto the rear yard. He pushed them outward and stepped across the threshold of the patio, drinking in the freshened air. Beth came and stood behind him, just inside the house.

"What time is it?" Bram asked, not turning around.

"About seven. Come inside and sit down, Bram. You must be exhausted. Do you want something to eat?"

He obeyed, shutting the doors after him. "No food," he said, gesturing for her to join him. "Just you."

He sat in the deep chair he'd occupied before, and pulled Beth onto his lap. When she settled against him his sigh was so long and so broken that it sounded almost like a sob.

"Your heart is beating," Beth said, putting her ear against his chest.

"I hope so," he answered, a smile in his voice.

The rain increased in volume, pounding on the roof, filling the twilit room with a dull roar.

"Bram?"

"Mmm?"

"Everything is going to be all right."

He didn't answer. When Beth sat up to look at him he was asleep.

She curled up again, sliding her arms around his waist. She was tired, too, and as she listened to the sound of the rain her eyelids became heavy.

In minutes she had joined him in slumber.

They were awakened abruptly by the sound of raised voices in the hall.

"I told you that you can't come in here," Mrs. Harkness was saying. "I was instructed not to admit anyone."

"I'm not *anyone*," a feminine voice answered. "I'm his wife."

Beth jumped up and looked at Bram, who lurched to his feet also, struggling to come awake. From the look on his face, he had recognized the voice.

The door opened and Anabel strode through it, followed by an agitated Mrs. Harkness.

"It's all right, Mrs. Harkness," Bram said quietly, eyeing their visitor. "I'll handle this. Thank you."

The nurse, obviously relieved to get out of the line

of fire, rushed from the room. Anabel surveyed Beth and Bram, her lovely eyes calculating.

"A charming picture," she said, examining their deshabille. "I hope I haven't interrupted something."

"What are you doing here?" Bram demanded. Beth had never heard that tone from him before; his voice was cold with new, unprecedented fury.

Anabel walked past them, touching objects in the room. "A pity you never let me touch this library," she observed. "I could have done so much with it."

Beth watched her, taking note of the peach wool suit, the perfectly matched shoes and bag, the exquisite jewelry. Anabel's champagne-blond hair was shorter than Beth remembered it, and done in a current style, a mass of shimmering gold. She was carefully made-up, her sea-green eyes accented with just a touch of shadow, her lipstick a creamy harmony with the color of her clothes. Beth knew that she had to be in her forties, but she looked years younger, and as beautiful as ever. Her portrait must be aging somewhere, Beth thought darkly.

"You haven't answered my question," Bram said. Every line of his body was rigid with tension.

"You know what I'm doing here," Anabel said lightly. "My husband is ill."

"You have no husband," Bram said flatly.

Anabel's coquettish demeanor changed instantly. "I'm still married to him," she stated coldly.

Bram nodded slowly. "I see. Now I know why you're here. You want to be first in line to get your hand in the till." He took a step toward her. "Listen, honey, I know all about your live-in boyfriend down in Florida, so don't try to pull the concerned-wife act with me. If I have to give it all away, lady, I'll see that you don't get a thin dime."

"My lawyers will have something to say about that," Anabel snapped.

"This is my lawyer," Bram replied, jerking his thumb at Beth. "And she'll have something to say about it, too."

Anabel's eyes flashed to Beth. "Your lawyer?" she inquired, and then smiled derisively. She walked slowly to Bram, and Beth could see the potent sexuality of her attitude toward him, her gestures. She put her hand on his arm, displaying manicured, melon-colored nails.

"Come on, sonny, don't be mean. I've come all the way from Palm Beach, and you're treating me like a leper." Her eyes caressed him. "You used to like me."

Beth wanted to strike her. She imagined Bram trying to resist this onslaught at seventeen, with a younger, more sensuous Anabel, and felt sick.

Bram pulled back from Anabel's touch as if it had defiled him. "I never *liked* you," he spat furiously. "Go back where you came from; your arrival is premature. My father is not dead yet, and if I can possibly help it, he will not be. Leave. I'll deal with you when I have to, and not before." He turned his back on her.

"You were always afraid to deal with me," Anabel said softly, a tiny smile playing about her lips. "Weren't you?"

Bram whirled around to face her, his expression murderous. "If you are not out of this house in two minutes, I will break your neck," he said between his teeth.

Beth believed him. She was moving to put herself between them when Anabel spun around quickly and left the room. She believed him, too. Seconds later the front door slammed so hard it echoed to the back of the house.

Bram went immediately to the liquor cabinet, taking out a glass and splashing scotch into it. He downed it in one gulp, his hands shaking.

Beth followed him, standing aside as he drank, and then moving closer to him to touch his shoulder. It was as hard and unyielding as granite. He wouldn't look at her. He had withdrawn again.

He replenished his drink, taking another large swallow. Then he glanced at Beth.

"I guess you gathered from that little scene what the problem between Anabel and me was," he said, in that self-mocking tone Beth hated. "She never was very subtle."

Beth didn't answer.

He smiled bitterly. "Nothing to say? Cat got your tongue? Well, I don't blame you. It's not a pretty picture. I wanted her, that viper, that gallon of poison. I wanted her, my father's wife."

"Bram, don't talk about it," Beth said weakly.

"Why not?" he asked, saluting her with his glass. "Doesn't it conform to your heroic picture of me?" He leaned in toward her, grinning. "That's what I've been trying to tell you, sweetheart. I'm really not a very nice guy."

"Bram, you were sixteen, seventeen, whatever. Boys at that age are confused enough about their sexuality. It must have been awful to have her at you all the time, taunting you. Don't blame yourself. You didn't do anything, you left home rather than do anything."

"But I wanted to!" he whispered fiercely, raising a finger in the air. "God, I wanted to. I used to lie awake at night in a sweat, picturing her just down the hall. . . ."

"I don't want to hear this," Beth moaned, turning away.

"Makes you sick, doesn't it? Well, it made me sick, too. I never started it, mind you. She was always coming on to me. That's what I told myself, later, so that I could live with it. But she knew how I felt, she knew she was getting through to me. It was clear that it was only a matter of time, so I got the hell out of the house, away from her and away from my father."

"It was the only thing you could do," Beth said. But she knew she couldn't comfort him; he was irrational in this mood.

"Was it?" he asked. "My father never thought so."

"Your father didn't know what was going on!" Beth replied, her voice rising. "Listen, Bram, you have to stop this. It's over now, and none of it was your fault. You're driving yourself crazy, and me, too."

"You don't like it?" he inquired, raising his brows. "Get out."

Beth stared at him, unable to believe he'd said it.

"You heard me," he went on, looking away from her. "Go home."

"Bram—"

"Go serve a writ or something." He drained his glass.

Beth stood rooted, unmoving.

"Still here?" he sneered, glancing backward. "I'm surprised. Now that you know all about me I was sure you wouldn't want to stick around."

He bent his head, blinking rapidly, and she realized suddenly that he was trying to get rid of her, fast, because he was on the verge of breaking down. He would do anything, say anything, rather than have her see that.

"I won't leave you," she said, her tone heavy with sympathy.

It was the wrong thing to say. "Don't feel sorry for me!" he shouted, throwing his empty glass against the wall. It shattered noisily.

Beth recoiled, her hand covering her mouth. "I only want to help you," she whispered.

"You can't help me. No one can help me. You've done your good deed for the day, go back to chasing ambulances."

Beth gasped. This was too much. He had no reason to take his unhappiness out on her; she had done nothing but show him kindness. She loved him, but she was nobody's carpet. Not even Bram was going to walk on her.

Beth ripped the bracelet he had given her from her arm and threw it at him. "Fine," she said coldly. "And you can go back to chasing secretaries." She ran from the room, grabbing up her things on the way, and dashed out into the rainy night.

The man is impossible, she told herself as she drove home, choking back the sobs rising in her throat. He's a maelstrom of conflicting emotions, a powder keg ready to explode at a moment's notice. Who needs it?

The hell with him. He could drink himself to death for all she cared, and drive everyone away from him with his ruthless sarcasm. He wasn't going to abuse Beth Forsyth any more.

Unfortunately, this resolution did not make her love him any less.

10

The next day Beth called Jason Raines. For weeks he'd been asking her to accompany him on a business trip to Hawaii. He was interested in purchasing several condominiums on the island of Maui and wanted Beth's advice on the contracts. He was leaving that night. She had been saying that she didn't have the time, but now she changed her mind. There was nothing really pressing that couldn't wait for a few days, and so she told him that she would go with him. Beth reminded him that it would be business only, and Jason laughed, saying he'd accepted that long ago.

Beth hung up the phone thinking that she needed to

get away. She needed to get away from Bram. The timing of this venture was ideal.

Mindy had called to say that Joshua was improving slowly but steadily, and was expected to live and make a good recovery. She'd called the house and spoken to Mrs. Harkness. Beth didn't ask about Bram, from whom she'd heard nothing since she left him in his library the night before. She couldn't bear to think of that final scene with him and so concentrated on other things. She hired the part-time secretary Mindy had recommended, left the woman installed in her office with the piles of records and correspondence, and went upstairs to pack.

When she came down two hours later she heard the reassuring clacking of the typewriter coming from the office. The pace of the sound was very encouraging; by comparison with Beth's hunt-and-peck style, Mary Margaret typed with the speed of light. Beth checked her purse for the necessities, and then glanced at her watch. She had an hour and a half to meet Jason at the airport in Windsor Locks, about twenty minutes away. She twisted her hair into a bun at the back of her neck, fastening it with pins. All in all, she thought she was coping very well for a woman whose world had crashed at her feet the previous evening.

Mary Margaret looked up briefly at Beth's entrance and nodded as Beth gave her the house key and told her to let herself out when she was done. Beth told her to keep track of her hours and submit a bill. She was Hal's friend, and presumably trustworthy; if she padded her bill or robbed the place in Beth's absence, Hal's judgment was not the monument of wisdom it had proved to be in the past.

Beth decided to leave and get something to eat at the airport lounge. The house was stifling her; everything in it reminded her of time spent there with Bram. When she walked out the front door and headed for her car she felt as if she'd been released from prison.

The phone rang in Beth's office about ten minutes after she left. The secretary picked it up automatically.

"Attorney Forsyth's office," she announced crisply.

There was a stunned silence from the other end of the line. Then Bram's voice said sharply, "You're not Beth. Where is Beth?"

"Miss Forsyth is away. May I take a message?"

"Away! Away where? And who the hell are you?"

"I'm Miss Forsyth's secretary. If this is a personal call, perhaps you might like to try the house line and leave a message on the machine."

"I already tried the house line, why do you think I'm talking to you? Since when does Beth have a secretary?"

"I was hired this afternoon. If you leave your name I'll make sure Miss Forsyth returns your call."

"Lady, you'd better tell me where Beth is. Right now."

"Sir, I see no reason to take that tone with me."

Bram thought rapidly, deciding to try a different tack. "Ma'am, this is Abraham Curtis, Miss Forsyth's fiancé. I apologize for my rudeness, but it's very important that I locate Beth and I'm anxious. Could you please tell me where she is?"

Mary Margaret thought that over. Miss Forsyth hadn't said anything about being engaged, but then, why would she? Would a stranger call her office with such an outrageous lie? The man really did sound upset. She wouldn't want to be the cause of any misunderstanding, but wouldn't a fiancé know where his future wife was going? She stared into space, undecided.

"It's urgent that I get in touch with her," Bram added.

The woman sighed. "Miss Forsyth is on her way to Hawaii. Her plane leaves from Bradley at eight. You can probably catch her if you want to go there."

"Hawaii!" Bram shouted.

"Yes, with Mr. Raines," the secretary continued nervously, already regretting her decision.

"With Jason Raines!" Bram yelled, and crashed the phone back into its cradle.

In Beth's office, Mary Margaret hung up the phone with the fixed conviction that she wasn't going to have this job very long.

Beth was waiting in the ticket line with Jason when Bram descended on them like a flash flood, grabbing Beth's arm and hauling her out of the group.

"Bram!" Beth gasped, astonished. "What are you doing?"

"I'm taking you out of here," he announced grimly, dragging her toward the exit.

"You are not! Take your hands off me!" She yanked her arm out of his grasp and glared at him.

"See here, Curtis, I think you misunderstand . . ." Jason began.

Bram jammed his forefinger under Jason's nose and barked, "You. Shut up."

Jason blanched. He shut up.

Beth glanced around at the staring crowd, mortified. "For heaven's sake, Bram. You're making a scene," she hissed.

"Do you think I give a damn? If I have to tie you to the ticket counter I'm going to make sure you don't go anywhere with anyone but me."

Beth sighed. She would have to talk to him or he would carry on until she did. She looked at Jason, who clearly wanted no part of this fiasco.

"I'll wait for you in the coffee shop," Jason said. "The flight isn't until eight."

"She won't be on it," Bram called after Jason's departing figure.

Beth looked for a secluded corner and found it in a nook near the water fountain. She hurried over to it with Bram on her heels.

"What on earth is the matter with you?" she demanded, whirling to face him. "That man is a client. Excuse me, he *was* a client. I'm sure he'll be looking for a new lawyer after witnessing your insane performance; he probably thinks we're both deranged. How dare you storm in here, pushing me around, acting like a . . ."

"Lover?" Bram suggested, his eyes flashing.

"Lunatic," Beth concluded. "How did you know where I was?"

"Your secretary told me. I've been running all over the place, trying to find the right airline. How could you even think of going away with that guy?"

"It's a business trip, Bram."

"Hah! So he's telling you. He's been after you all along, everybody knows it."

Beth closed her eyes, trying to stay calm. "Bram,"

she said, striving for a reasonable tone, "the last time I saw you, you insulted me and acted like a brute. Now you show up here, throwing your weight around, asserting rights you don't even have."

"I have every right in the world. I love you."

Beth opened her eyes. He'd said it, but not in the way she'd anticipated. Instead of the moonlight and musical background she'd imagined, she had the stark air terminal lighting and the blaring of the loudspeaker. Bram was not kissing her hand or looking lovingly into her eyes, he was glaring at her, his fists planted belligerently on his hips. Something was wrong with this picture.

"Did you hear what I said?" he asked.

"Yes, I heard it," Beth replied faintly. "Forgive me if I don't throw myself into your arms."

Bram sighed, pressing his lips together. "Okay. Look, I know I have a lot to answer for, but I can't explain anything if you don't give me the chance. Please stay, Beth. We'll go someplace and talk. Please?"

Beth met his eyes and couldn't resist the mute appeal she saw there. She nodded silently.

His brow cleared instantly. "Wait here," he said. "I'll go and tell Raines."

"Bram, don't . . . do anything to him."

Bram shot her an exasperated look. "I'll spare his life at your request, fair lady," he said, and Beth had to smile. She sat in a nearby chair and tried to convince herself that she wasn't making another drastic mistake.

When Bram came back he steered her toward the doors leading to the promenade. "I booked us a room at the airport hotel," he said. "I thought we could talk there."

Beth stopped walking. "Confident, weren't you?" she said.

He halted, too, looking down at her. "No, mouse. Just hopeful."

She searched his face and saw that he was telling the truth.

"Shall we go?" he asked softly.

"Yes," Beth replied, following him outside.

The hotel room was filled with flowers. Baskets and vases overflowed with red roses. The heady perfume washed over them like a wave as they entered.

"Do you like them?" Bram asked eagerly, watching her face.

"Of course. Who wouldn't? Such an extravagant gesture, Bram; it's just like you. Nothing by half measures, right?"

He didn't answer.

"I'm overwhelmed, as you intended," Beth added.

"I did the wrong thing," Bram said dully.

"No, but . . ."

"But?"

Beth licked her dry lips, wondering if she could possibly make him understand. "Bram, you can't expect to walk all over me one day and then romance the hurt away the next when you feel better. Women have been letting you get away with that behavior far too long."

He sagged against the closed door. "No sale, huh?" he sighed. He walked to the bed and sat on its edge, putting his head in his hands. Every line of his body bespoke disappointment and defeat. "Don't give up on me, Beth," he whispered. "Please."

Beth approached him and put her hand on his bent

head. The thick, springy hair, as black and shiny as polished onyx, curled about her fingers with a life of its own.

"I could never do that, Bram," she said quietly. "I love you much too much."

He sighed deeply, not looking up, then put his arms around her, hiding his face in the folds of her skirt. "I'm sorry, Beth," he murmured, his voice muffled by the clinging material. "Forgive me."

Beth knelt beside him, forcing him to sit up and look at her. "I do forgive you, Bram, but I don't understand you. I know how difficult yesterday was for you. It must have been horrible to find your father so ill, with all that had gone wrong between you, then to have to face Anabel at the same time. Her arrival was obviously the last straw. But instead of leaning on me, sharing with me, you *turned* on me. You made me the target, the outlet for all that hostility. It wasn't fair, Bram."

His brown eyes, shot through with gold at the irises, dropped away from hers. "I know that," he said hoarsely. "I was up all night last night kicking myself for saying those things to you."

"Why? Why did you do it?"

He stared at the floor, still avoiding her gaze. His lashes, long and spidery, as black as his hair, fanned against his cheeks.

"I never wanted you to know about Anabel," he said in a low tone. "I never wanted anyone to know, but especially not you. After she made that scene, I felt . . ." he paused, curling his left hand against his chest in a gesture expressive of the depth, the intensity of his emotion. "I felt . . ." he said again, and stopped.

Beth grasped his hands in both of her own. "You felt what, darling? Tell me."

"I felt ashamed," he said. "I mean, it's so apparent what she is, what she *was,* and yet I let her come between my father and me, I let her disrupt my whole life and drive me out of my own home. I was such a fool."

"Bram, you were just a boy."

"I let her get to me. And I didn't want you to see that, I didn't want you to know that she was the reason I left. She wasn't worth it then, and she certainly isn't now."

Beth took his face between her hands. "Bram, listen to me. You have to let this go. Your father is getting better, and you've already started to rebuild your relationship with him. I know that Anabel is going to cause trouble in the future—she left no doubt about that—but she has no power to hurt you anymore. I'll be with you; we'll fight her together. You won't be alone."

Bram pulled her into his arms in a quick, fierce motion, pressing his lips to her hair. "I don't want to be alone," he said softly. "I'm so tired of being alone."

Beth closed her eyes in thanksgiving. She knew that this was hard for him to say, even more difficult than admitting he loved her.

He held her off and surveyed her, his eyes shining with happiness—or a suggestion of tears—Beth couldn't be sure. "I have something for you," he said. He reached into his pocket and produced the mouse charm, dropping it into her palm. "I had the chain repaired."

Beth closed her fingers around it. "I'm sorry I broke it. I have an awful temper."

"The outburst was justified," Bram answered. "I have something else, too. I picked it up while I was at the jeweler's. I thought I'd kill two birds with one stone." He produced a small, velvet-covered box from his other pocket, handing it to her.

"Open it," he urged, when Beth simply stared at it.

Her heart pounding, Beth lifted the cover. On a bed of royal-blue velvet sat a sparkling, pear-shaped diamond.

"You had this when you came to the airport," she said.

"Of course."

"What would you have done if I'd refused to listen to you?" Beth asked.

"Kill myself?" he suggested, sounding like he was only half kidding.

Beth looked up from the ring to meet his eyes.

He shrugged. "I guess I would have waited until you got back and then tried again."

"Even if you thought I was having an affair with Jason?"

He lifted one shoulder slightly. "I gave you reason enough to turn away from me. And I'm the last person who should sit in judgment of anyone about that."

Beth dropped the box on the rug and flung her arms around his neck, bursting into tears.

He held her close for a few seconds, and then said, tentatively, "Does this mean you'll marry me?"

"Yes, yes, yes," she replied, clinging to him. "I've spent a third of my life waiting to answer that question." She burrowed into his chest until her sobs subsided, and then drew back to examine him. Bram tilted her chin up with one hand and wiped the wetness from her cheeks with the other thumb.

"My most precious mouse," he murmured. "I don't deserve you."

"That's true," Beth responded. "But I love you anyway."

He laughed, and kissed her lightly. Beth kissed him back eagerly, and he pulled her onto the bed with him.

"We might as well use this room," he muttered, his kisses trailing to her neck as he unbuttoned her blouse.

"Certainly, if it's paid for," Beth answered, holding his head against her. "We wouldn't want to waste the money."

He undressed her in record time, slipping off the bed to shed his own clothes. When he lowered himself on top of her he groaned with satisfaction.

"Oh, Beth, I love you so much," he whispered. "Why did it take me so long to realize that?"

Beth didn't get a chance to reply. His mouth covered hers and she was lost in a world of sensation.

Beth woke to hear Bram ordering a bottle of champagne from room service.

"What are we celebrating?" she inquired when he got off the phone.

"The night I finally grew up," Bram said, settling back and drawing the blanket around her shoulders.

"Hear, hear."

"You don't have to be so smug about it."

Beth giggled. "Sorry." She yawned and stretched. "I guess I dozed off."

"I guess I wore you out," Bram replied in a dry tone.

"So when are we getting married, Mr. Curtis?" Beth asked.

"Whenever you want."

"We have to establish a few ground rules first."

Bram groaned and pulled the sheet over his head. "More ground rules?"

"Yup."

He sighed dramatically. "Okay. Let's have them."

"No more running off to sea."

"Absolutely not. Everything I need is right here."

"No more drinking and getting into fights."

"I'm taking a solemn vow of abstinence right now," he said, raising his right hand so that it indented the sheet above his head.

"No more withdrawing from me when you're upset."

His draped head nodded back and forth.

"And no more visits from Gloria at your house."

He whipped the sheet off and flung it away from him. "Now wait a minute. I draw the line right there."

Beth punched his arm.

"Ouch. Gloria is my secretary. Sometimes I bring work home."

"You're not bringing that kind of work home anymore."

He grinned. "Okay, boss. I guess I'll just have to transfer those duties to you." He grabbed her and pulled her on top of him.

"Bram?" Beth said, resting her head on his shoulder.

"Yeah?"

"What will happen to poor Gloria and poor Dr. Reynolds now? Not to mention that poor station manager and whatever other poor women you've been seeing."

"Lots of poor ladies in Suffield," he commented.

"Answer the question."

"Well, I suppose they will observe a suitable period of mourning, the usual sackcloth and ashes, maybe a funeral wreath or two. Then, if they try hard enough, they will probably be able to recover and lead full, productive lives."

"You are insufferable."

"You asked me," he said, his eyes widening.

There was a knock at the door. Bram pulled on his pants and answered the summons, returning with a bottle in his hands.

"I thought you were giving that up," Beth said.

"I'll start tomorrow." He popped the cork and poured the wine into two bathroom glasses, giving her one.

"To us," he said, raising his high.

"I'll drink to that," Beth replied, and touched her tumbler to his. They both drank deeply. Bram climbed back into bed, juggling the bottle and his glass.

"Do you suppose there's a reckless moon tonight?" Beth asked.

Bram looked at her, smiling slightly. "Where did you get that expression?"

"You told me about it, the night of my father's party. Don't you remember?"

"Did I? God, what a memory you have."

"I think I remember everything you've ever said to me."

He set his burdens on the end table, turning to her and taking her glass out of her hand. "I don't know about a reckless moon in the sky, but there is a reckless man in this bed." He dropped her glass on the rug.

Beth smiled at him. "And a reckless woman, too."

"Then we're a perfect match."

And, with her cooperation, he proceeded to prove it.

WIN

a fabulous $50,000 diamond jewelry collection

ENTER

by filling out the coupon below and mailing it by September 30, 1985

Send entries to:

U.S.
Silhouette Diamond Sweepstakes
P.O. Box 779
Madison Square Station
New York, NY 10159

Canada
Silhouette Diamond Sweepstakes
Suite 191
238 Davenport Road
Toronto, Ontario M5R 1J6

SILHOUETTE DIAMOND SWEEPSTAKES
ENTRY FORM

☐ Mrs.   ☐ Miss   ☐ Ms   ☐ Mr.

NAME   (please print)

ADDRESS   APT. #

CITY

STATE/(PROV.)

ZIP/(POSTAL CODE)

RTD-A-1

RULES FOR SILHOUETTE DIAMOND SWEEPSTAKES

OFFICIAL RULES—NO PURCHASE NECESSARY

1. Silhouette Diamond Sweepstakes is open to Canadian (except Quebec) and United States residents 18 years or older at the time of entry. Employees and immediate families of the publishers of Silhouette, their affiliates, retailers, distributors, printers, agencies and RONALD SMILEY INC. are excluded.

2. To enter, print your name and address on the official entry form or on a 3" x 5" slip of paper. You may enter as often as you choose, but each envelope must contain only one entry. Mail entries first class in Canada to Silhouette Diamond Sweepstakes, Suite 191, 238 Davenport Road, Toronto, Ontario M5R 1J6. In the United States, mail to Silhouette Diamond Sweepstakes, P.O. Box 779, Madison Square Station, New York, NY 10159. Entries must be postmarked between February 1 and September 30, 1985. Silhouette is not responsible for lost, late or misdirected mail.

3. First Prize of diamond jewelry, consisting of a necklace, ring, bracelet and earrings will be awarded. Approximate retail value is $50,000 U.S./$62,500 Canadian. Second Prize of 100 Silhouette Home Reader Service Subscriptions will be awarded. Approximate retail value of each is $162.00 U.S./$180.00 Canadian. No substitution, duplication, cash redemption or transfer of prizes will be permitted. Odds of winning depend upon the number of valid entries received. One prize to a family or household. Income taxes, other taxes and insurance on First Prize are the sole responsibility of the winners.

4. Winners will be selected under the supervision of RONALD SMILEY INC., an independent judging organization whose decisions are final, by random drawings from valid entries postmarked by September 30, 1985, and received no later than October 7, 1985. Entry in this sweepstakes indicates your awareness of the Official Rules. Winners who are residents of Canada must answer correctly a time-related arithmetical skill-testing question to qualify. First Prize winner will be notified by certified mail and must submit an Affidavit of Compliance within 10 days of notification. Returned Affidavits or prizes that are refused or undeliverable will result in alternative names being randomly drawn. Winners may be asked for use of their name and photo at no additional compensation.

5. For a First Prize winner list, send a stamped self-addressed envelope postmarked by September 30, 1985. In Canada, mail to Silhouette Diamond Contest Winner, Suite 309, 238 Davenport Road, Toronto, Ontario M5R 1J6. In the United States, mail to Silhouette Diamond Contest Winner, P.O. Box 182, Bowling Green Station, New York, NY 10274. This offer will appear in Silhouette publications and at participating retailers. Offer void in Quebec and subject to all Federal, Provincial, State and Municipal laws and regulations and wherever prohibited or restricted by law.

SDR-A-1

READERS' COMMENTS ON SILHOUETTE DESIRES

"Thank you for Silhouette Desires. They are the best thing that has happened to the bookshelves in a long time."
—V.W.*, Knoxville, TN

"Silhouette Desires—wonderful, fantastic—the best romance around."
—H.T.*, Margate, N.J.

"As a writer as well as a reader of romantic fiction, I found DESIREs most refreshingly realistic—and definitely as magical as the love captured on their pages."
—C.M.*, Silver Lake, N.Y.

"I just wanted to let you know how very much I enjoy your Silhouette Desire books. I read other romances, and I must say your books rate up at the top of the list."
—C.N.*, Anaheim, CA

"Desires are number one. I especially enjoy the endings because they just don't leave you with a kiss or embrace; they finish the story. Thank you for giving me such reading pleasure."
—M.S.*, Sandford, FL

*names available on request